Advance Praise for

"Philip Roth may have p   t
before siring a love child o   ....ct David Kalish,
whose exuberant, hilarious first novel uncovers the light side
of divorce, cancer, and computer dating. Sharp-tongued yet
warm-hearted, Mr. Kalish shows us that the opposite of everything we know is exactly what we've needed to learn."

—Askold Melnyczuk, *The House of Widows,*
Ambassador of the Dead; founding editor, *Agni Magazine*

"*The Opposite of Everything* is an evocative tale of pre-hipster
Brooklyn in which Mr. Kalish injects his pitch-perfect humor
into some of the most challenging quandaries a career-focused
New Yorker can face. His oddball characters mix in a clash
of cultures between native New Yorkers and the immigrants
who infuse the city, and the book's central character, with
new life."

—Gerry Mullany, deputy editor, *The New York Times*

"Mr. Kalish's first novel is a wonderful book. I can't help but
compare the protagonist, Daniel Plotnick, to the very best of
John Irving and Philip Roth's quirky and unforgettable characters. This book will have you laughing out loud, and that
Plotnick himself would believe is excellent for your health."

—Virgil Suarez, *Latin Jazz, The Cutter, Spared Angola*

"Kalish knows these people intimately, and he tells their tale with heart, grace, and a journalist's clear eye."

—Will Hermes, *Love Goes to Buildings on Fire: Five Years In New York That Changed Music Forever*

"A comedy about cancer? A love story about divorce? David Kalish's debut novel *The Opposite of Everything*, is the opposite of everything you'd expect in a book with these downbeat themes. It's a grand toast to contrarian optimism and a grand cheer to Life!"

—Aimee Liu, *Cloud Mountain, Flash House*

"A zany, romantic novel about the things that break our hearts—cancer, crazy families, and busted dreams—and the things that sustain us: love and second chances."

—Seth Kaufman, *King of Pain*

"David Kalish's first novel is rich with hilarious cultural clashes. He's taken meaty chunks of his life, thrown them into a stockpot with a Colombian blend of spice, and added a dash of kosher humor. All in all, an intimate and joyful delight."

—Becky Lyn Rickman, *The Convict, the Rookie Card, and the Redemption of Gertie Thump*

The Opposite of Everything

The Opposite of Everything

Everything

a novel

David Kalish

*To my favorite rabbis,
and good friends,
Jonathon and Linda,*

David Kalish

WiDō Publishing
Salt Lake City • Houston

WiDō Publishing
Salt Lake City, Utah
www.widopublishing.com

Cover Design by Steven Novak
Book Design by Marny K. Parkin

ISBN: 978-1-937178-43-7
Library of Congress Control Number: 2013958278
Printed in the United States of America

I dedicate this book to Ingrid and Sophie, for believing in me even when I didn't. And to my mother and father, who stood by me in real life.

Chapter One

ERE'S HOW IT STARTS. FIRST, A PERSON HAS HIS health. Heart. Relatively easy commute. Decent career. Sense of humor. On occasion, he eats a Big Mac for lunch. Half a pint of Ben & Jerry's before bed. A general optimism pervades his Brooklyn neighborhood, outdoor cafes vying with baby strollers for sidewalk space. Then one morning he wakes up—and concludes the only way he'll live another day is to do the opposite of everything that came before.

Daniel Plotnick woke up.

It was April 1996, shortly before 7 a.m. Squinting into the light, he glanced across the bed sheets at his wife, Judy, and felt a pain in his neck.

An actual lump in his throat.

His groans woke her. She stared at the swelling in his neck and reassured him it should fade on its own. She compared the lump, right near his Adam's apple, to a pimple inside her nose that goes away. Like a sudden thunderstorm, it should abruptly give way to sunshine. He tried to convince himself she was right. The young couple, after all, was married four months—too soon, presumably, for major hiccups. But the next day, Plotnick's family physician weighed in against his wife's rosy assessment. After examining the lump, he advised a battery of tests, and referred him to a higher-level doctor who, in turn, diagnosed Plotnick with the condition that would ultimately send him, and his life, into literal free-fall.

At first, the newlyweds clung to optimism. And why not? After determining Mr. Plotnick had thyroid cancer, his surgeon—a stoop-shouldered old-time practitioner they'd shopped long and hard for, with floor-to-ceiling walls of certificates and diplomas, hands reputedly steady as clams—said if you're going to get cancer, thyroid is the one to get. Ninety percent cure rate! After removing the thyroid (a pale bilateral butterfly of a gland the doctor intoned, nearly waxing poetic, whose metabolic function is easily replaced by a once-a-day pill) infuse the patient with radiation and—voila!—any stray cancer gets zapped.

And so Plotnick went under the knife to remove his thyroid, a vocal nerve, and a sliver of trachea, not to mention fifty-two lymph nodes in and around the neck, with the belief he was curable. He kept his chin up during his week in the hospital, barely able to swallow or talk, staples knitting together his grimace-shaped gash, and another week in bed at home with ice packs and painkillers. He clung to the word "curable" like a life preserver and, two weeks after surgery, nature itself seemed to throw him one.

That afternoon, as Judy drove him to Long Island for his post-operative checkup, Plotnick turned his sore, bandaged neck to see out the window. Spring was breaking out in Brooklyn! Greening boughs arched overhead like parade banners, dogwood buds were exploding into white popcorn puffs, robins tweeted, and pansies dripped like molten gold from window boxes off the sides of brownstones. Through the open door of a bakery, the aroma of freshly baked rolls wafted past his nose.

Renewal was in full bloom: Plotnick expected *his* winter was on the wane.

Because—miracle of miracles!—he had the curable kind.

"Spring's finally here," he told Judy in his raspy voice, the tumor having damaged his left laryngeal vocal nerve.

Judy gazed up from the road to meet his glance. Her eyes—even his wife's eyes—seemed a deeper shade of green.

"Thank God," she agreed, and went back to watching the road.

His wife pulled off the highway and parked; Plotnick eagerly staggered out. Inside the clinic, however, the surgeon who'd brimmed with confidence behaved oddly. He ushered them into his office and sat stiffly across from them. Operative reports sheeted his desk, and when he looked up from them, his eyes were gray and troubled.

"Now Mr. and Mrs. Plotnick, there's something we need to discuss," Dr. Douglas said from behind his desk. "Frozen sections of the thyroid excised during surgery came back from pathology. I'm afraid the diagnosis has changed. We thought the cancer was curable, but I'm sorry, it isn't."

Plotnick, sitting next to his wife, swallowed to coat his dry throat, his Adam's apple bobbing uneasily under the gauze swaddling his neck. The words sounded eerie and disturbing to him and, by force of habit as a journalist, he tried to distract himself with less catastrophic usages. *Bacon is cured,* he mused. *But there ain't no cure for the summertime blues!* Still, Plotnick's inner wordy-gurdy didn't help much, and he felt beads of sweat spring across his forehead.

"What do you mean he's not curable?" Judy asked, her voice tightening in sync with her grip on Plotnick's hand.

Dr. Douglas reiterated he'd been prepared to dose Plotnick with radioactive iodine to mop up any cancer remaining after the operation. But his condition—medullary thyroid carcinoma, as it turned out—originated from a part of the thyroid that doesn't "take up" iodine. "Frankly, I was caught off guard. Because the cancer is sporadic, there's no traceable cause, no genetic predisposition or event like cigarette smoking that might have triggered the cells going haywire." The doctor rubbed his eyes tiredly. "Honestly, it's like getting hit by lightning."

"Maybe I should play the Lotto," Plotnick said, drifting from the conversation. Hadn't he been a long-distance runner with zero history of serious illness? "I'd be a millionaire with so much luck."

"Daniel, be serious," Judy said, but seemed to build on this subject of odds. "What are his chances, doctor?"

Plotnick tried to turn a deaf ear and look away, twisting his achy neck best he could, but Dr. Douglas's words broke through loud and clear. Speaking patiently and firmly, he said folks with this particular condition are given a fifty-fifty chance of surviving ten years, but then added the caveat about statistics being meaningless. He gave the expected advice to live each day with meaning. After all, Mr. Plotnick's cancer was slow-growing—except when it behaved badly.

"You should proceed with your life. Both of you. Mr. Plotnick could have ten years, or fifty. You could be run over by a truck sooner than the cancer gets you. So, take time to enjoy!"

Chapter Two

PLOTNICK MET HIS WIFE THREE YEARS EARLIER in Times Square. It was 1993, before New York City banned smoking in bars, and he'd sat alone nursing his beer in the tumorous haze, after a long day covering business news for the Associated Press.

Rubbing his tired eyes, he strained to see the clues in a *New York Times* crossword puzzle. A shapely woman sidled near, in a black cocktail dress, having come from a Christmas office party with a friend. He was struck by her gypsy green eyes, made mysterious by dark long lashes, and her smile of evidently corrected teeth.

"Six-letter word for what are you drinking?" he remarked. She commented, later, how he resembled a slacker version of Steve Jobs, whom she greatly admired, with his rimless intellectual glasses set tight across a hawk-like nose.

Before long the two fell into conversation over pink, complex drinks about Nietzsche, Harold Pinter, and Mayor Giuliani's bad toupee, how last month it blew off in front of TV cameras on the steps of City Hall, dominating the five o'clock news, even in China.

Like Plotnick she was in her early thirties and a voracious reader (she worked as a librarian), and they enjoyed a common ethnic cynicism. One Friday after work, he visited her place in Borough Park, a Jewish neighborhood on the other side of Brooklyn from his Park Slope. Evening was descending. He gazed out her apartment window at bent old women and men hurrying down the sidewalk, limping as fast as they could to get to the kosher butcher before it closed at dusk, or to a minion, the ten-men minimum required for a prayer service. This pre-Sabbath scene, she insisted, made her think of a Russian shtetl during the time of Cossacks. "Of course, the shtetl comparison is flawed," he countered, as they cozied up on a sofa, sharing a bottle of Manischewitz. "All these tall brick buildings would seem out of place in a tiny Jewish village a hundred years ago in Eastern Europe. Where every mother wore a shmata and had at least ten kids."

"Yeah, but Borough Park still smells like chicken soup and matzoh balls. You know what it's like meeting guys around here? Not exactly an aphrodisiac. The smell is, like, forever."

The rabbi who married Plotnick and Judy commented at the altar how healthy they appeared, hand-in-hand before God. A sinewy jogger, Plotnick squirmed proudly in his vanilla tux. "Good health and marriage go hand-in-hand!" the rabbi intoned in the reddish glow of the ceiling-high eternal lamp, as if the Higher Authority himself were blessing the rabbi's assessment.

Mere months later, though, the doctor's prognosis trumped the rabbi's.

⟡   ⟡

As Judy drove them back that afternoon from the doctor's visit—speeding down the highway, it would later seem to him, as if trying to get home before something else went wrong—Plotnick gazed gloomily out the passenger window, seeing the opposite of what he'd pictured merely an hour earlier. He noticed not the perfumed flowers but the potholes in the road and graffiti slashing the sides of buildings. He heard trucks rattling and whining down the pocked streets, he smelled their exhaust fumes and—as they reached their Brooklyn neighborhood of Park Slope—sensed a cloud descending darkly over the outdoor cafes, all the writers and artists and other cool people, it seemed to him, letting their Lithium prescriptions lapse.

"Penny for your thoughts, Dan." Judy reached over from the driver's seat to touch his hand.

Had he been a more expressive person, Plotnick might have shared a couple of things. About how he already missed what might no longer be. How he'd hoped to pen a novel, in the not-too-distant future. Perhaps become a foreign correspondent, searching for adventure in exotic lands. How he wanted a couple of kids to look up to him. They'd all live in a spacious suburban house instead of the claustrophobic fourth-floor walk-up in Brooklyn, sow seeds in a little garden plot, weed the tomato plants, and set down aluminum pie plates filled with Budweiser to drown the slugs. One day, Plotnick had hoped to retire with a full pension. But right now he didn't feel much like talking—to Judy, or anyone. Especially about things that might not come to pass.

"Danny?"

"Yeah?" he said, fiddling with his glasses.

"Raise it to a quarter for your thoughts."

"I'm not thinking anything," he said, softly, not caring if she heard him or not.

❦   ❦

The only thing worse than being declared incurable, Plotnick realized in hindsight, were Judy's attempts to cure him.

It was a few days after his neck bandage came off; Plotnick sat slumped at the kitchen table taking a stab at *The Sunday Times* puzzle, trying to distract himself from the futility of it, from the inept medical profession, from all those high-paid physicians who seemed no more effective than a witch doctor rattling dried seeds over a comatose snake-bite victim.

Judy burst through the door laden with grocery bags. He glanced up. The sun, coming low through the window, slanted crazily across her pink flushed face as she removed item after unfamiliar item from the bags and set them before him on the table. She pulled out handfuls of dark green leaves. A jar labeled "flax." A half-pound of green tea, a bag of wheatgrass, three vials of primrose elixir, ground up almond butter with natural oils. She'd weighed out pumpkin seeds, pine nuts, dried pomegranate. The kitchen filled with the ripe odor of vegetables and nuts and fruit on the verge of turning. Plotnick gazed back down at the crossword puzzle to divert his attention from the hub-bub, but a large kale leaf blocked the Across clues.

"We need to talk," she said, grabbing the crossword from him.

Plotnick threw his pencil to the table in frustration. Couldn't a man with a death sentence do the puzzle in peace? But Judy set down the remainder of her purchases, put up a pot of green tea, and for the next fifteen minutes paced the room and spoke. She told him she had found herself, literally and figuratively, in the largest health food store in Brooklyn.

"Like I almost lost consciousness. I mean the answer was right there in front of me!"

"Answer to what?"

She ignored the question and bull-dozed onward to tell of her feeling of self-blame that had its roots in girlhood—a feeling very much like oops! At the age of nine-and-a-half, playing in her basement, Judy clumsily jump-roped through a house she'd built of toy wooden blocks for her pet hamster, crushing its furry little body. Even though it was an accident, her mother, a member of PETA, banned her from owning a hamster ever again. Things worsened when Judy became old enough to drive, which was shortly after her mother rescued a cat from the animal pound. Backing out from the driveway one moonless night in her mother's car, she heard a brief but desperate feline squeal. By then head of PETA for the entire Northeast, her mother revoked her car privileges and gave her the evil eye until she was twenty-one. Afterwards, whenever someone in her life became gravely sick or died—a dog, say, or a grandparent—Judy felt as if she'd committed a punishable act. She felt like the kiss of death.

As Plotnick listened, his fingers worried his scar. The story sounded, frankly, like one of those crazy stories you hear on Dr. Phil. "I'm surprised you never told me this before, Judy," he said. "How long have you had these issues?"

Sniffling, she handed him back the crossword puzzle and grabbed a tissue. "If you must know, I didn't bring it up sooner because I didn't think it was relevant. It sounded so stupid, besides. But then this incurable thing happened. I know intellectually I didn't *cause* you to get sick, of course, but psychologically…"

"Aloe!" Plotnick blurted out, scratching in the word.

"Are you listening?"

"Of course. My brain works on two levels." Plotnick put down the pencil and held up his hand like a traffic cop. "Judy, listen to me. Much as I respect Freud and Jung and that whole fruitcake profession, this isn't about you, or them. *I'm* the one who had the operation. This hamster thing happened, like, twenty years ago. No reason to let guilt eat you up."

Judy stared at him. "I get what you're saying, Daniel. But you need to understand what I'm saying too. My condition and your condition ... we're made for each other!" Everything in her life up to this point, she went on, felt like practice. It was bottom of the ninth, two strikes, two outs. Gripping the bat handle, she stared hard at the pitcher motionless on the mound, a pitcher who threatened to strike them out. Turn their lives into a cosmic joke. A joke that began, like so many, in a smoky bar. A woman gazes into a stranger's eyes, lets him buy her a drink. Existential philosophies and phone numbers are exchanged. After several adventures, she hitches a ride on his star. But the star goes nova.

Judy resumed cramming vegetables and grains into the refrigerator and closets.

"I still don't get what you're doing with all this stuff," he said, gazing blankly at a box of gluten-free pasta.

"Five-letter word for plant-based balm."

"Er, aloe has four letters."

"Five-letter word for plant-based balm," she repeated. "I'm trying to speak your language, Mr. Puzzle Man."

"Wait ... got it! V-E-G-A-N."

She nodded at him supportively, as if he were a toddler taking his first jerky steps. "To help you recuperate," she said in a nurturing way. "To make sure everything doesn't become a joke."

He took a moment to do the math. "Fifteen letter word for 'I still don't get it.'"

"Listen, buster," she said, "vegan is part of a cleansing diet that strengthens the liver and purifies the body of free radicals to reinforce the immune system. And your immune system desperately needs reinforcement to fight those stray buggers surgery missed. Now which syllable of 'vegan' don't you understand?"

Chapter Three

JUDY, HE LATER RUED, WAS TRUE TO HER WORD. She served up bland meals of tofu, flax, wheat grass, and the like. She prepared green tea by the pitcher. Packed his lunchbox with bean sprout and hummus sandwiches on sprouted wheat. He picked and sipped and made faces. She bought him a book, *The Liver is the Center of Things,* for its enema-centered program of "organ detoxification."

He felt himself grow defiant. One evening he brought Judy to a French restaurant in Manhattan to "loosen you up," as he put it, but she hardly touched her plate, waving away wine. By then, he'd grown a patchy beard. She nibbled on red snapper; he shoveled in veal stew. She coldly eyed his dessert, a floating island of meringue in a pool of brandy-flavored custard. "Impeccable!" he declared, dabbing his lips with a napkin. He sipped his espresso (an intestinal inflammatory) in silence.

"You really don't get it," she said, by now a common refrain of hers, as the white-gloved waiter splashed Cointreau in his sugar-rimmed goblet.

"No, I don't," he replied, sipping possible poison.

Instead of vegetables, he gravitated toward White Castle and chicken wings. Drank more beer than he should. Instead of going directly home from work, he took to dropping by a bar in Alphabet City after putting in his nine or so hours at the Associated Press as a business reporter. His pal Steve Kirsch, a Bell Atlantic repairman during the day, managed the place part-time while moonlighting, when necessity struck, as Plotnick's de facto therapist.

It was late afternoon in July; Plotnick's bandages were long off, scar fading into pink. He sat at the bar, staring blearily at the lit-up liquor bottles. Steve came over, his goatee still white at the tip where he'd singed it a few nights earlier exhaling a spray of 151 at a lit match, shooting out a cone of fire to entertain drunken customers.

Steve poured without asking, slid a cold one to Plotnick, and pensively rested his singed chin in his hand. He was squat, chin hairs struggling to make up for a dearth on his scalp. A regular guy yin to the neurotic Plotnick's yang, he seemed to lack a neck. "You look terrible," Steve said.

"And you look like you just got back from the burn unit," Plotnick said, referring to Steve's crisped chin. "You work like a hooker here."

"With freeloaders like you, D, gotta make money somehow." Steve watched impatiently out the smudged front window at a truck rattling past. "Listen. Enough with the banter. This place could get busy any minute. So start venting already. You look sick with worry."

"Who are you, my nurse?"

"Nah. I'm more like Robin to your Batman." Steve reached behind the counter and poured his own. "So start talking."

"Well, if I did say something, and I'm not sure I will, it would be you have no idea what it's like being married."

"Finally he speaks."

Plotnick pulled out a bag of carrot sticks sprinkled with wheat germ his wife had packed. "Look what she's doing to me!"

"What's wrong with carrots?"

"It just makes me mad. I'm not sure why. Okay? Like she's trying to squeeze blood from a stone."

"You being the blood or the stone?"

"Just blood from a stone. Isn't that enough?"

Steve shaved the foam off his beer with a martini stirrer. "Go on."

"You want to know my method?" Plotnick said. "To *not* focus on the buggers the surgeon may have left in me. I don't want that kind of stress. Thing is, I feel better. The cancer's not bothering me right now. The scar's healed. I could have a better chance of getting hit by a truck than dying from cancer. Of course, we don't live near any major truck routes...."

Plotnick took a tragic swallow of beer. "But here's the thing. Every time I turn around she reminds me I'm sick. With *these*." He waved the carrot sticks in the air. "I mean, here I am trying to get on with my life. And she's feeding me tofu chunks!"

"Refill?"

"Sure."

Steve went around the counter and poured another. "Want my advice? Talk to her in a language she understands. Tell her your guts are like badly insulated electrical wires, and if she keeps touching them the wrong way they'll fry her brain by accident. Trust me on this. I'm a phone technician."

"How would some electrical analogy enlighten her? Help her see I want to move on? I mean, I have a decent career as an editor and reporter. A healthy 401K. Used to run marathons. Though of course I had my fast-food binges, who doesn't? Nothing I couldn't run off the next morning—"

"You're babbling."

"—all the time thinking that fat and sugar could be neutralized by an extra hundred or so slaps of my cushioned soles against Brooklyn asphalt. If my body could get it together to slog twelve miles on a Sunday morning, then it could certainly keep some renegade cells from busting out all over. This is what I once thought."

"Come on guys!" Steve announced to the nearly empty room, as if speaking over an imaginary PA system to all ten trillion healthy cells of Plotnick's. "It's you against them!"

Plotnick stared into his beer. "If only she understood."

"Let's see. Maybe tell her cancer is like when one phone wire skitzes out and sends signals all over the place to places they should never go. The wire shorts out of the blue, or something makes it go short, like water, or fire."

"Have you heard nothing I said? Judy is freaking out! How would some ridiculous comparison help her freak out less?" He sighed. "I just want her to leave me alone."

"Well, you're here. That's not alone. What am I, chopped liver?"

They went way back. Steve was the sort of guy who showed up, which is what he did three months earlier. There they were, Plotnick and his family, gathered in the waiting room of New York Hospital in Queens, waiting to see him off for his neck operation, back when everyone still thought he had the good kind. Plotnick sat wedged in his blue gown between his divorced father and mother on one side, an ashen-faced

Judy on the other. His mother and father sat rigid as statues, on their best behavior, straining not to bicker with each other. Once in a while his father would get up to check the hall clock because he had a date that evening and hoped to meet her in Chinatown on time.

Suddenly Steve walked in from his day job in his Bell Atlantic jumpsuit, utility belt strapped with unfamiliar tools, holding his motorcycle helmet. Plopping down across from Plotnick, Steve snapped his gum and announced, "Feels like a freakin' London wax museum in here." He placed a meaty hand on his buddy's shoulder. His minty breath wafted past. "Tell you a little story. Other day I'm up a telephone pole testing the phone for a customer in Brooklyn. I dial his number. Some woman from Akron, Ohio picks up. I ask, 'Is this 555-1111?' She replies, 'No, this is 555-1112.' I tell her: 'Oh, I'm so sorry for disturbing you.' And you know what she said? This old lady says, 'It's all right. I had to get up to answer the phone anyway—!'

"Here's the moral," Steve said into the confused silence. "The lady had to get up to answer the phone anyway. Get it? She made the best of a bad situation. So what someone dialed a wrong number? Someone *always* dials a wrong number. *Life* is a wrong number. But you pick up the phone anyway. You answer the damn—"

"Daniel E. Plotnick!" a nurse called out from the other end of the room, jerking everyone's attention.

Plotnick reluctantly stood. Steve, one of the few in the world who knew what the 'E' stood for, grabbed his buddy's arm. "No matter what, you get on with the conversation. You make a joke out of it. This is the message I got from the old lady. This is what I'm trying to say."

"Thanks, Hans Christian Telephone Man. But it's not like you're seeing me off to my first day of kindergarten," Plotnick said, as Steve continued to grip his arm. "It's only a simple operation to rip open my throat."

"Kindergarten was a long long time ago, bro."

"I bet they didn't even have caller ID back then," Plotnick said, misty-eyed.

Steve opened his hand, releasing him to the nurse.

By the time Plotnick left Steve's bar, several beers later, evening had descended on the city. Plotnick stumbled through lamp-lit East Village streets, past tattoo parlors and dive bars. He noticed, as if for the first time, teenagers and twenty-somethings slumming on stoops and in alleys: in black garb with hair to match, faces pale as death. Instead of standing out, these rejects blended in with the shadowy neighborhood. Plotnick felt an odd camaraderie. He could see something similar happening to him: blackness bathing him in a kind of negative luminescence, like the warm waters of a Jacuzzi under a moonless night sky.

Plotnick's wordsmith side received a good workout that evening. On the subway home from the East Village, he inwardly riffed on the hard g of goth; not the pussy-whipped first letter of giraffe or gee wiz, but the iron-clad confidence of go!, geckos (able to scale sheer walls without blinking), and gargantuan. Not to mention, g was the last letter of nose ring.

Goth, by definition: medieval, uncouth, barbarous. Its mere sound soothed him.

Still later, Plotnick staggered in drunk through the door of his apartment. He donned a coal-black shirt cut short at the sleeves like a tank-top. Instead of regular sleeves, dark denim sheathed his arms: evidently something stitched together by an East Village designer high on pot. His shoes were Doc Martens, the over-priced, high-top, black-as-night leather footwear for overly image-conscious Bohemians.

Clopping into the kitchen for a glass of water, he nearly tripped over Judy, who sat on the floor stabbing a spoon at a pint of Häagen-Dazs.

Husband and wife gasped roughly at the same time.

"My God!" she said, wiping stray drops of ice cream from her lips.

"Well, this is new information," he said, staring at the pint in her hand, feeling sober.

"Er, are you dressed undercover for a hacker's convention?"

Exasperated, he thudded his briefcase to the floor. "You see," he explained, "I'm exploiting my darker side. The universe is made of matter and anti-matter, and right now in this specific moment, I'm anti."

"Wow, this really clarifies everything," Judy said, eyeing his black get-up. "Where'd you get all this crap?"

"Just something I picked up downtown after work. There was a sale in the East Village."

"The entire East Village was having a sale? Couldn't the Gap be having a sale? And, you're *drunk*. Hanging out at Steve's bar again? He's a bad influence, serving you alcohol. What kind of friend does that? Does he care if you stay healthy? Look at the result. You come home dressed like a cat burglar. Like you're about to sneak past me and hide."

He pointed to the pint in her lap. "Who's hiding what from whom? Here you are trying to force-feed me squirrel food while you sneak in Häagen-Dazs. Isn't that a felony or something?"

"It's whatever crime you want it to be." Sniffling, she turned her back to him and put the half-finished pint back in the freezer. "I'm going through a hard time, Daniel. I mean, with you sick and me not doing anything about it. You could at least *try* to help me help you instead of getting so dark." She blew her nose. "I used to be a yo-yo dieter. Okay?"

She'd never told him this information before. Coming after the hamster revelation, it was his wife's second admission in three months of something strange and disturbing hidden inside her. It was roughly around this time, moreover, he noticed a related phenomenon: his wife was gaining weight.

In coming weeks, Judy took to wearing large-size blouses, shapeless as potato sacks. The sight made him feel too weary and drained to say no when she suggested they drive to the Catskills for a free weekend get-away, courtesy of her mother's well-connected boyfriend. "Lots of sick writers recovered in the country," she urged, "or had their main characters recover there. Think of Thomas Mann. Byron. At the very least the fresh air will lift your spirits."

So on the morning of their first anniversary, Plotnick drove them the three hours north to the Nevele resort, a restless assortment of aging, leaky structures. Later in the day, they canoed down a swampy river swatting armies of mosquitoes and still later, drank non-alcoholic beer in plastic cups in the room where he managed, with some effort, to climax despite using an over-lubricated condom.

Still later as she slept, softly snoring, Plotnick searched a hidden pocket of his suitcase and pulled out a cigarette hidden there for special occasions. When was the last time he'd smoked a post-coital cigarette? Years! *If this cigarette kills me before cancer kills me, then maybe she won't feel so guilty about my dying.* His own deviant thought frankly surprised him.

Through the room window, horny crickets droned like a phone off the hook; the only constellations were the night noises, the bleating of frogs searching for mates. He blew a mournful lance of smoke through the screen. Shadows fled across Judy's body, his gaze resting on the expanse of her bare back. It was full of beauty marks he hadn't noticed before. They formed a sort of constellation, reminding him of something he'd once dreamed. A certain tranquility swept over him. A nostalgia for lost innocence.

Over the next few months, Judy's secretive binges intensified, she stored her smaller-sized clothes in mothballs, and he found himself grinding his teeth at the contradiction: the food his wife ate to numb the pain of guiltily watching him sicken was in fact making him suffer more. This tortured paradox, this interconnectedness of life and death, reverberated not merely through his brain but the entire neighborhood.

One morning on the way to the subway to work, all sorts of ironies spawned. He passed the office of Dr. Fingar, oddly a podiatrist, and spied an Alcoholics Anonymous upstairs from a wine store. In CVS he noticed cigarettes and snuff situated next to Nicorette and other anti-smoking products, aisles of candy and cookies and soda butting up against diabetes medications, condoms and Today sponges alongside pregnancy test kits. And so on. This evident conspiracy between life and death and the forces that would profit from it struck Plotnick with an urge to further test his gothic limits.

One evening after work he visited a tattoo parlor on St. Mark's, where a muscular pock-faced man with tattoos covering roughly seventy percent of his body, dominating his flesh like the oceans dominate the Earth, bored a small hole through Plotnick's nostrils.

That night he entered the apartment more drearily than ever. Judy was sprawled on the couch popping bonbons and watching some sitcom. When she saw him she abruptly turned off the TV. Her jaw dropped, and he pictured something squirming near her heart, as if one of those creatures from the first *Alien* movie were trying to gnaw its way out through chest bone.

"Daniel?" she said, stopping him in his tracks.

He set down his briefcase. "Yes?"

"That little pet snake you have crawling through your nostrils. What is it?"

"Oh. Herman."

"You've named it! How perfect!"

"Just kidding, J."

"Are you?"

"So what if I named it?"

"Seriously, aren't you afraid you'll lose your job?"

"I'm a reporter. We have a liberal dress code," he said, running a finger along the ring's smooth surface as if indeed stroking a pet snake. "Besides, people who discriminate against those with piercings follow dated stereotypes."

"Where'd you get that line, from the Idiot's Guide to Going Goth?"

He smiled at her with bemusement. "Listen. Go through what issues you need to go through. But this is all about me."

"No. It's about me too. First you go black and now, frankly, you look like you have a very shiny booger stuck to your nose. It's like you've *totally* given up on yourself." She breathed in and held it, as if suspecting she were about to hate herself. "Please don't take this the wrong way. But until you take that weird creepy thing off, you sleep in the living room. Just the thought is making my face break out with hives. You *know* how I'm allergic to silver. Remember what happened when you bought me a pair of silver earrings for my thirtieth birthday? My ears blew up like Dumbo's. My cheeks grew a strawberry patch!"

"Huh?" he said. "It's not like you have the ring! And you'd have the bed to yourself. And that's not fair. The living room is the farthest possible distance from the bedroom without formally exiting the property."

"I'm sorry, Daniel. Silver oxidant rubs off on bed sheets. Ask any metals expert. What do you think of sleeping in the kitchen instead? It's closer to the bedroom."

"You know damn well that's an excuse. What about *my* health? I'm the one who's sick. I'm the one with cancer!"

"Then why," his wife said in an oddly quiet voice, "do I feel like part of me is dying?"

Plotnick clasped his briefcase and went into the bedroom, slamming the door. He came out carrying his pillow, clock radio, and personal items to the living room, where his new bed, of all things, was a love seat. A short lumpy sofa.

It looked to him like the answer to a crossword clue: furniture piece stuffed with hypocritical meaning.

Despite protracted negotiations in coming weeks over sleeping arrangements and eating habits, their positions hardened. He ate out comfort food to cope and became a regular at McDonald's, brooding over Big Macs. She went for dinner at her mother's several evenings a week. At one point he suggested she move to her mother's for a few days to see how it went, since she was often there anyway, but she refused, saying she wasn't ready "to give up on you." The apartment slipped into silence, communications largely left to insinuation and notes taped to the refrigerator door. As he twisted on the love seat at night, his mind raced. *She can't handle my cancer. That simple. Just like she couldn't handle the dead hamster.*

Over time a voice from his inner editor drifted up. "D comes after C." At first he dismissed this statement as an obvious alphabetic fact. But after several weeks of trying to sleep on the ergonometric equivalent of a stale potato chip, something snapped in him.

Chapter Four

L ATE ONE NIGHT, AS MOONLIGHT PUSHED BACK the darkness through the window, Plotnick rose stiffly from the couch. Heart racing with trepidation, he flicked on a light and reached high into the hall closet, pulling out old medical scans of his neck and upper chest. He scattered them across the kitchen table under the overhead lamp. Through thick and thin, he'd kept them safely stowed in his apartment. What would these films of his cancer tell him now? He fingered the top sheet as if consulting a Ouija board, holding it up to the ceiling light. Gazing into the luminescence he examined the image of his pre-operative neck dotted with infected lymph nodes, before the surgeon cut them out. Plotnick drew back in wonder, realizing something: the images were photographic *negatives*. His old nodes glowed white against tracheal bone, white as stars in a night sky, instead of bloody dark spots against white bones, as he pictured his anatomy appearing in actuality. Likewise, the next CT scan held up to light showed Plotnick's cancer behaving the *opposite* of medical expectations. This particular scan was taken after surgery. Defying his doctor's prediction he could be cured, all the spots missed by the surgical knife shined brightly. They were non-curable, the opposite of treatable, because radiation was not an option. The surgeon had gotten Plotnick's prognosis wrong. The spots glared back at him with impunity. They couldn't be zapped.

Then and there Plotnick understood something. A message had been transmitted through the medium of his medical history.

The scans, a.k.a. Ouija board, suggested he do the opposite of what came naturally.

The first contrarian seeds were planted in Plotnick.

The next evening, when Judy was out at her mother's, he flipped through the "Attorneys and Agents" section of the North Brooklyn Yellow Pages. The act felt immoral. Dangerous. It went again his grain. He located a bearded, portly divorce lawyer, who lived and worked in a Park Slope apartment a few blocks from his. When he got there, he made a confession. He feared the stress of living with his wife was compromising his immune system. His wife refused to try separation. The lawyer, Harvey Udall, smiled with understanding and, based on his experience, assessed the marriage as beyond repair. He laid out a method he'd honed with numerous clients who, like Plotnick, sought to escape irreconcilable tension. He drew up a letter giving her a month and a half to vacate the apartment. Since Plotnick bought the place before the marriage, which presumably was of short duration, he legally owned it and could do with it as he wished.

The suddenness of the suggestion shocked Plotnick. "Isn't asking her to leave radical?"

"It's actually very generous," Harvey said. "Legally we only need to give her thirty days, not a month and a half. And you, my friend, can't leave the apartment, because she could claim you gave it up."

That night Plotnick handed Judy the lawyerly letter. Replying with action not words, she tore it up and swung her arm, swiping a shelf filled with tchotchkes. One, a porcelain statue of "The Stinker"—a pensive man sitting on the toilet, chin planted in his palm—grazed his ear and smashed against the wall, shards showering the floor. He delicately backed out of the apartment, fled down the stairs, and crashed at Steve's apartment that night.

Her response was clear. How dare he throw her out.

The next morning, gloomier than ever, he called in sick to work and returned to Harvey's office. Clearing off a table, the lawyer spread out a Rand McNally street map of Brooklyn, a yellow-lined legal pad and a freshly sharpened no. 2 pencil. He said authoritative and direct phrases such as: "Find out when spouse is not home." "Get a witness for the locksmith." "Call family member to lend you support." "Give spouse one hundred cash and tell spouse to find a place for the night. We're not bastards, after all."

His urge was to say no. Locking his wife out felt extreme. Wrong. It went against everything he'd been taught about marriage. Yet his heart needed immediate action. If he thought too much, he might chicken out, and his heart couldn't endure another day of living with a woman angry enough to toss tchotchkes at his head.

He remembered, for comfort, his medical scans—the starry night sky, the positive images of negatives—suggesting he go against the tide.

Locking his wife out was the opposite, he reassured himself, of his every moral impulse.

He returned to his apartment, nervous and dazed by what he was about to do. It was early afternoon—Judy out working at the library. On impulse, he dialed his father's phone number, seeking support in case the excrement hit the fan, reaching back to his nostalgic past for comfort. He hoped his old man could make room in his dating schedule. Plotnick clung to the ideal he'd always be there for his son, no matter how many women he was juggling.

His father picked up; Plotnick for the first time opened up to his old man about his marital problems, right down to the lawyer's suggestion about the locksmith. He told him his fears of Judy's reaction. Could he come over, like, in a few hours, to back up his son?

"Christ, you're going through a lot, kid. Be happy to lend a hand!" Harold Plotnick said through the phone. Of course, he added, he'd have to run it by Fiona.

"Fiona?"

"We have our regular dinner date in Chinatown. 7 p.m. Wo Hops. But first we're going to shop for lichee nuts at the market there. She's coming over my place—" He paused as if checking his watch. "—any minute."

Fiona. Wo Hops. Lichee nuts. Plotnick tried to process these bizarre words. "So you can't come over?"

"Don't distort what I said, Danny. I'd be happy to come over as soon as I work it into my schedule. Hey! I've got it." Plotnick heard the sharp snap of fingers through the earpiece. "It's already decided."

"Decided?"

"Instead of Chinatown, Fiona and me will eat in Sunset Park. They have plenty of Chinese there, and it's only fifteen minutes from your apartment."

"You're switching your restaurant plans from Chinatown to Sunset Park? For *me*?" Plotnick said, mockery creeping into his voice. "Say it isn't so."

"Sure. This way me and her will kill two fortune cookies with one stone."

"Wow, Dad. I don't know what to say!"

"Just say thanks. We'll be over your place with plenty of time to spare."

"We?"

"Me and Fiona, of course."

"Oh for Christ sake … this isn't a spectator sport, Dad."

"Fiona is open to new experiences. No worries as far as she's concerned," his father promised.

Plotnick's pulse quickened. He flashed back five months, to when another elderly man confidently told him "no worries." It was a week before his neck surgery: the surgeon gazed at him across the desk with clear bright eyes, saying, reassuringly, he had "no worries" thanks to radiation, which would surely mop up any cancer remaining after the operation.

It was all downhill from there.

"I'll ask Steve to come over," Plotnick, a bit winded by the memory, told his father. "It's going to be awkward enough as it is."

He heard the chime of a doorbell through the phone; his father said he had to run, presumably to open the door for Fiona, and asked Plotnick to let him know how it went. After his father hung up, Plotnick stared at the earpiece. He scolded himself for making the call. No, he'd fight his impulses from now on. Instead of blindly following his lawyer's advice, Plotnick resolved, he'd twist it one hundred eighty degrees.

Plotnick punched in Steve's number. Later that afternoon, after the locksmith left, he paced his living room in wobbly ovals, patches of sweat spreading from his armpits, the shiny new lock staring out from the door like an all-seeing, guilt-invoking eye. "You're making me dizzy," Steve said. He placed a comforting hand on Plotnick's shoulder. "Make the damn phone call already. Get it over with."

Plotnick nodded. He called Judy at her mother's, where she'd gone for dinner, and informed her he'd changed the locks. Speaking diplomatically and in general terms, seeking to appeal to her desire for his well-being, he noted that separating seemed like the best thing for his health, and the health of their relationship.

There was a dramatic pause on the line, then, "You changed the effing locks?"

"Er, yeah. But it's not what you…"

Judy slammed down the phone, producing an emphatic dial tone in his ear.

"…think." Plotnick hung up.

"How'd she take it?" Steve asked.

"She's probably coming over with her mother. If you think Judy's hard-core, you should see her mother. She once banned Judy from owning a hamster!"

"Why?"

"Judy accidently killed one. The mother's an animal rights fanatic."

"I see." Steve thoughtfully stroked his goatee. "This may be a bad time to bring it up, dude. But at least Judy's mother comes to help her. But your father—he blew you off for a chick! Hate to say it but he shows up when it's convenient. Pisses me off," Steve said. "You *asked* him to help you out."

Plotnick gazed out the window at the half-dark street below. "He made the excuse I could trust you to help me handle things, and you're solid. I agreed with him there. And I suppose he did offer to help me out. In his own way, he wanted to be here."

"Yeah. But your father's second childhood is interfering with your first adulthood," Steve said.

"Yeah. His post-divorce schedule is interfering with my pre-divorce schedule."

"What are fathers for?" Steve slapped him on the back. "You'll do *fine.*"

"Sure I will," Plotnick mumbled, even as doubts clouded his mind—doubts even his best buddy couldn't know about.

Fifteen minutes later, the friends heard a car squeal up, red lights flashing urgently across the window. They simultaneously gazed down through the glass panes at the street four stories below. Two cops stepped out of a squad car. Plotnick's wife and mother-in-law emerged from the back.

The buzzer sounded to the apartment.

When Plotnick opened the door, unlocking the new deadbolt, the pair of white cops stared back at him like disapproving bookends, on either side of a steaming mad mother-daughter team. Steve stood shoulder-to-shoulder with his friend. For a long awkward moment the six of them lingered in the doorway getting the feel of things. Plotnick's heart hammered against his chest. If Hannibal could sneak forty elephants and fifty thousand men across the Alps in three weeks flat to defeat the Romans, he strained to reassure himself, maybe he could do the Brooklyn version.

"Ahem!" the bigger cop said, gaze darting between Plotnick and Steve. "Which one of you gents is Daniel Plotnick?"

"*He* is," Judy said.

"I see. Mr. Plotnick, did you change the locks on your wife?"

"Yeah, he did! He told me he did!"

"Sir, you can't lock your wife out of the marital abode. You got to give her what, forty days notice?"

"Thirty," the shorter cop corrected.

But Plotnick handed them a document drawn up by his lawyer. It bore an official court stamp. In a dazed nervous way he knew his arguments were solid. His lawyer had found a Brooklyn family judge to agree, in half a New York minute, with Plotnick's paradoxical contention he could legally give up his home.

After skimming the papers, the cops gazed down the stairs—as if dreading a Kathmandu-sized mountain of paperwork piling up on their desks into the wee hours. For a long moment they said nothing.

"What's going on?" Judy's mother asked, peering over at the document.

"This is what's going on." Plotnick picked up a suitcase he had waiting by the door. He reached into a pocket and dropped the new set of keys in Judy's hand. "I'm locking myself out. Going to live with Steve so I won't feel guilty about locking you out." He handed her one hundred dollars in cash. "So I won't be needing this."

"What!" Steve exclaimed. "You didn't tell me this. This is the opposite of what I—"

"Exactly," Plotnick muttered. "It's precisely the opposite. This is why I'm doing it."

"Do you get this, Bud?" the taller cop asked the shorter. "He's locking *himself* out."

"No, Pat. I'm sure I don't get it."

The policemen scratched their hats; the taller cleared his throat. "Ahem. Why don't you grab what you need for now, Mr. Plotnick? Pillow, underwear, that sort of thing. Blender. You can arrange to pick up the rest of your stuff at a later date."

"What great news!" Judy's mother said.

"Look at it this way, Judy," Plotnick said. "We need to break up before death do us part. I hope you understand. This is the best thing for my health. For both of us. It's time for you to stop suffering over me. So I can stop suffering too."

Judy was silent. "I'm not so sure," she finally said. "You *need* your place to come home to. Your familiar surroundings. How else are you going to get…" Her voice broke off. "This is so crazy. Why do you have to be so freakin' kind all of a sudden? You're killing yourself with kindness!"

"Judy, dear, take what's being offered to you," her mother said, giving her a little shove into the apartment. "Recognize a gift for what it is."

But Judy stood her ground against her mother, face twisting with indecision. A calm seemed to wash over her. She dropped the keys in Plotnick's hand and faced him. Her green eyes glistened. "No," she said. "You're staying. I'm going."

"Excuse me?" her mother said. "Judy! You're being handed a gift here!"

Judy dropped the hundred dollars in her mother's hand. "No, Mom. I know exactly what I'm doing. I'm going to live… with you. It's the only way I can truly help him heal."

Steve's jaw dropped, as did the mother-in-law's.

"Okay," the big cop said to Judy, "*you* can arrange to pick up your items at a later date."

Judy pecked Plotnick on his cheek and began down the stairs, her flummoxed mother and the cops still standing there at the top, not moving. After three steps, though, Judy walked back up and peered into her husband's face.

She held his hand. Smiled kindly. "I understand what you mean, Daniel. We need to break up before death do us part. I am *that* dear to you."

"To each other," he corrected.

"Go heal," she suggested. "For me." They hugged. She extracted her hand from his, turned, and went down the dimly lit stairway, followed by her distraught mother and the amazed cops.

Gazing down after them, Plotnick could imagine the rest. Pushing open the door to the street, Judy would squint into the afternoon. So bright, yet muted. A warm breeze kissing her face. Greening boughs would arch overhead like parade banners, dogwoods explode into popcorn puffs, robins tweet, and pansies drip like molten gold from window boxes off the sides of brownstones. Aroma of warm bread wafting past. Spring was breaking out in Brooklyn; Judy would expect *her* winter was on the wane. And so she'd catch the next subway back to Borough Park and, upon moving in with her mother, would recheck the newspaper obituaries on a daily basis to confirm her husband remained among the living.

And that, in short, was how Plotnick came to christen his new contrarian approach. In one swoop he'd regained his apartment and his peace and quiet. As an added bonus, his soon-to-be ex didn't want to kill him. Naturally, he still felt haunted by his failures. Nights, he staggered home from Steve's bar, drew the blinds in his newly bachelor bedroom and laid back, seeking oblivion. To ease his mind, he inserted his ear buds and pressed play on his heavy metal music.

Death's in my bones like a bad disease! He kills me each time he lays eyes on me!

Electric guitars screeched as if in great pain; Plotnick distractedly worried the scar across his lower neck. At one point, he thought he heard a ringing but ignored it. Plotnick raised the volume a little more, to block out the ringing.

He eventually fell asleep, but his angst returned in a recurring nightmare. He dreamed he was flat on his back in an open field surrounded by bleachers filled with on-lookers in doctor uniforms. His wife stood demonically gazing down at him through a surgical mask. Plotnick heard a crackling. He glanced down and saw his own chest crack open—a baseball-sized tumor floated up through his splintered rib cage and hovered, spinning, spattering blood across his wife's face as she moved her prayerful hands across it, her voice rattling some ancient chant. Applause erupted, a bit too cheerfully, from the medical crowd in the bleachers.

But one day, through the clapping of those hands, Plotnick again heard that other sound. Brring! It caught him unawares. Brring! Brring! His eyes jerked open; he was drenched in sweat from the terror of his dream. He robotically picked up his glasses from the night table, placed them across the bridge of his nose, and touched his nose ring for comfort. He pushed a lock of hair out of his eyes.

Brring! Brring!

Plotnick reached as if in a trance for the phone on the night table.

"Yeah?" he answered, realizing his mistake too late.

"Christ, are you alive!" Then, more calmly, "Well, how have we been, Danny?"

"Oh, hi Dad. How have I been? Trying to sleep. But the phone keeps ringing."

"Sleep? Why are we sleeping at lunchtime?"

"I find a nap helps me when I don't sleep all night."

"Helps us do what? Not answer the phone for three days?"

"We? Us?" Plotnick felt stricken by these words. "Are we part of some larger community of minds?"

"Listen. *I* know you're going through a tough time, Danny. *I've* been there. What's it? Seven years I'm split from your mother? I have conditions too—an ulcer and arthritis in six fingers... anyway this isn't about *me*. For Christ's sake, at least tell me how you're doing after the showdown with your wife. The one I'm sorry I didn't make."

"How am I doing? This is how I'm doing." He ejected the CD from the Discman and inserted it into the music player in the living room. Harsh electronic sounds emanated from the speakers.

His father was forced to raise his voice through the phone. "You're doing construction noise? Listen, an idea. Enough with all this phone tag. Why don't you come over to my place for a few days? Get away from all this nonsense."

"Not to get technical, but you don't call it phone tag if you're the only one playing."

His father didn't reply for a moment, evidently absorbing his son's rude comment. Plotnick turned up the background music, as if texturing an especially violent movie—the shower scene, say, from *Psycho*—not merely to drown out his father, but his own unease with disrespecting him.

"Why are you so angry with me, Danny?" Harold yelled over the music.

"Your priorities disgust me. I could have been arrested but you were more worried about Kung Po Chicken."

"Actually, I prefer Beef with Broccoli. But don't you see, Danny? I want to make it up to you now. I'm back in the saddle!"

It was then Harold proposed to "really make it up" to his son—by taking him to the Catskills for an old-fashioned singles weekend and get him "back in the game." The idea had disaster written all over it. Danny could get lucky with Medicare recipients! Dance disco with women in walkers! His impulse was to not even flatter his father with a reply and hang up, slamming down the phone.

But then he thought about it. Like Siddhartha, the forefather of Buddhism who staggered through a desert of deprivation before achieving consummate tranquility, Plotnick could choose the more difficult path. Like Gandhi, who starved himself to free the Indian masses from their colonial masters, Plotnick could suffer discomfort to achieve ultimate transcendence. Besides, how much worse could he feel? He felt like a stand-in for Japan getting hit by an earthquake and tsunami roughly at the same time. The analogies grew tiresome. The one-two punch of divorce and disease will do that.

"What do you say?" Harold asked into the chaos of his son's thoughts. "I can't wait here all day for an answer. Fiona asked me over for lunch!"

Plotnick pressed the buds back into his ears, raising the volume.

Then he hung up the phone.

Chapter Five

DEEP IN HIS BOWELS, HAROLD PLOTNICK KNEW he was a good match for his son. Harold harbored his own demons, a witch's brew of emotions with the potential to bring out the worst—or the best—in his son. He hoped the latter, but feared the former.

After his son hung up the phone on him, for instance, Harold anguished over the rebuff. He poured some heated milk from a pot on the stove. He pushed a shock of white hair out of his eyes, sat on a kitchen stool, and sipped, waiting for his stomach to calm. He purposefully removed his reading glasses as if the act of focusing up-close hindered him from seeing something in the distance, some larger truth.

Harold gazed out his living room window at gray fomenting ocean. The violence of waves. He remembered. He remembered his own divorce from Danny's mother. Those last waning days of marriage, his habit of sleeping on a pull-out couch in the den, trying to separate from his wife without actually moving out. How one gray winter morning he awoke to the moist, smelly, bruising sensation of an entire pail of kitchen trash getting dumped on him and across his make-shift bed—chicken bones, coffee grounds, a nearly empty jar of Deaf Smith's Organic Almond Butter (still dripping with nut oil!) and the like. He could still picture his ex-wife's face grinning like a mad Cheshire cat through the gloom, urging him to "take yourself out with the garbage, Harry." Not coincidentally, the lease on the one-bedroom apartment he'd been contemplating in Coney Island commenced a week later.

Kid's going through a tough time, Harold thought, staring into his milk, nearly surprised to see his own reflection in the shimmering circle of white, and not his son's. *Just like I did. Even worse.*

Even worse because of me.

Harold determinedly dialed again. And again.

And his son finally agreed to go. Sure, it required more convincing—about five more phone calls. In the end Danny frankly sounded too drained to argue back. He related how a divorce judge ordered him to pay ten thousand dollars to Judy to compensate her for the loss of her home. It emptied his bank account, and wiped the last bit of guilt from his heart for locking her out. What with divorce and disease, he told his father, "dancing with female Medicare recipients would be the final debasement of me. Sure I'll go!"

For years after, the memory of their trip up would remain vivid in Harold's mind: cool morning air rushing through the open top of his aged Mustang, old fart music crooning through the car player. It was shortly after Tax Day, a time of new beginnings (at least to Harold, a retired CPA), as he drove up the spine of upstate New York in the lime green convertible he'd picked up used shortly after his own divorce. There was a spring in his pedal foot, and he was nearly surprised to see the speedometer registering sixty-five mph, the speed limit on the New York State Thruway, a full ten mph faster than his usual. His mood, if not his humming, felt in harmony with Sinatra's "I Did It My Way" through the car player.

Harold briefly lifted his gaze from the road toward his bony-framed darkly dressed kid in the passenger seat. Never mind that his Danny repeatedly wrinkled his nose with distaste (causing the ring through his nostrils to wriggle like a shiny worm) as he hunched over the glove compartment thumbing through cassette tapes of Englebert Humperdink, Tony Bennett, and the like. Never mind a bright pimple marked the fleshy hole where the ring went in. Or his hair had gone to black from brown since the last time his father saw him. None of this counted anymore because Danny Plotnick—miracles of miracles!—sat right where his father could keep an eye on him.

And what was going through his father's mind? Precisely this: If a whole generation of second-rate comedians could succeed in the Borscht Belt, his ailing newly divorced kid should be a cinch.

For nostalgia had a way of softening things, opening Harold up, welding his present to a honey-coated past. And their April road trip held such promise! He drove buoyantly on and on into the Catskills, neither of them speaking much. After seventy miles or so of zero conversation, Danny fell asleep, and Harold spied his Adam's apple gently bobbing, mouth cracked open, a fish-gut of saliva connecting his lips. A faint whistle coming through his nose ring. He eased the car off the NYS Thruway and onto Route 17, the squiggly asphalt aorta into the green heart of the Catskills. Harold opened the convertible top to let the rush of minty pine air cool his teeth and gums.

"Lookit this will yah!" Harold said out loud (to himself, for his son still slept), as the Mustang brushed swathes of fields, acres of winter wheat waving momentously as if welcoming Odysseus home from his ten-year journey following the fall of Troy.

The road curved sharply past a wooded pasture. As Harold craned his neck to see, cows wrapped in maps gazed ironically up as if seeking direction—transporting him back to a time when the dark stains of their hides seemed maps to an imaginary universe. For cows had been printed on the wallpaper of Danny's boyhood room, and there were also cows in the fields Harold had passed driving his family to the Catskills every summer in the late 1960s and early 1970s.

The vista hadn't changed much from those road trips, more than twenty summers earlier, when the three would meander up in a red 1967 Dodge Dart; or, when that conked out, a yellow AMC Gremlin. Danny strapped in back playing the "Ghost" spelling game with Harold at the helm, father and son munching on salted nuts they passed back and forth, Eleanor worriedly checking the maps. Verdant fields and mountains going on and on through the windshield, like there was no tomorrow. And today, in fact, was tomorrow.

True, the old haunts seemed more run-down, more windows since boarded up and barns collapsed and charred in splintered heaps, but the names hadn't changed—towns like Cairo, Goshen, and Florida, evoking a forgotten, nearly Biblical past. And Esso was still a brand! As his son slept, Harold cruised into this Esso station lined with clunkers, got out, and, as in yesteryear, he wasted quarters in a red Coke machine shaped like an old rounded Frigidaire.

With much persistence he bought a cold one. "Nothing like Coke in a glass bottle!" Harold said, waking up his son in the front seat, and perhaps it was progress he said nothing sarcastic, did nothing but accept the bubbly elixir his father offered, touched the bottle rim to his lips and drew from it. Harold felt similarly grateful when some geezer with a sucked-in mouth, who presumably ran this same Esso station, whistled through his teeth and mistakenly asked the son, not the father, how much he'd sell the Mustang for. Harold winked knowingly, as if to say, *You're sitting on a pot of gold, kid, get used to it.* And the kid, to his credit, made no rude facial gestures back.

Harold ramped back onto Route 17 and, by pleasant habit, raised the volume on another Sinatra standard, "Strangers in the Night." His son's hand edged toward the player as if considering something. Then, evidently thinking better of it, he adjusted back his seat and shut his eyes. "Good thing I brought my Six Dead Bolts," Danny said matter-of-factly, patting the rectangular bulge in the pocket of his dungaree jacket.

Harold threw a glance at his son. "Just a question. Why would you bring hardware to a singles weekend?"

Chuckling, he took out the CD from his pocket and held it up. "No, Dad. Six Dead Bolts. It's my head banger music. My enema for this weekend."

"I see! Don't mean to force my tastes on you, kid. But these women like romantic music, not construction noise."

"Yeah, but at least they don't need to turn up their hearing aids to hear it."

Harold lowered the volume on Sinatra in order to make music a less contentious issue. "Danny, you have acid in your voice. Why did you agree to come if you're so bitter?"

"I got tired of your pleading messages on my answering machine?"

"Guess this could be a reason. I think I left about fifteen. But why are you so angry with me?"

"I think you know why, Dad."

Harold sighed. "How many times can I say I'm sorry? Don't you see? I'm making it up to you now."

"Sometimes it's too late for sorry. And it wasn't the only time." Danny gazed out at the bucolic scenery passing by. "Forget it, Dad. The world feels like a conspiracy to me. This is where my head's at. Let's move on. I mean, I'm here, right? Mind if I play one of my CDs instead of your thirty-year-old cassette tape? Unless you own Metallica."

"Er, the CD part is busted so the car only plays cassettes," Harold lied.

"I shouldn't have let you talk me into this. This is all wrong."

"Forget about the music." Harold turned off the Sinatra altogether. "What do you say we talk? Me and you. The important thing is you're here. Even if you've changed a bit since the last time I saw you. I mean, now you've got this ridiculous black get-up, hair dye, a nose ring, and a taste for music that sounds like steel beams being ripped apart. But this last part I blame on your mother."

"You see," he said, staring through the windshield with lost eyes, "I'm exploiting my darker side. The universe is made of matter and anti-matter, and right now in this specific moment, I'm anti everything. This way, everything bad feels normal to me. I'm catching up to all the losers in the world. So please, Dad, let me be a loser."

His son glanced away; Harold had the good sense not to goad him further and so no more words were spoken during the ride up. The Mustang plunged deeper and deeper into the Borscht Belt, passing faded and warped signs for Catskills resorts long since closed and abandoned, and finally a somewhat less faded one announcing the Guttenberg. A heart-shaped poster dangled down, announcing the weekend's main event, "Last Chance to Rekindle Romance!"

As the Mustang entered the grounds, the sweeping unkempt lawns and hulking structures dating back to the Catskills' heyday nearly half a century earlier, Harold tried to counteract his anxiety about his son with memories of recovering his own heart in this very same Guttenberg Resort and Hotel—itself a survivor of hard times.

He took his first singles weekend here not too long after his divorce from Danny's mother. How the women had flocked to him! Back then he was in his mid sixties: the male-female ratio was pretty good, with far more men than women in his age group getting knocked off by heart attacks, strokes, cancer, and the like. Harold felt lucky to be one of those male survivors during his first weekend back in action, which gave him a taste for dating three or four women at a time (though when he returned to Coney Island, his dinner and movie expenses forced him to cut back).

Harold swung the Mustang in front of the resort's main office, thinking, *Could Danny also benefit?* He wasn't sure: the formula for recovery certainly wasn't fool-proof. Even after plunging back into dating, he'd felt haunted. How many times had he sat across from some faux redhead or blonde at a nice restaurant when he'd stiffen up over his chicken parmigiana, spaghetti dangling in mid-air from his fork? Just by gazing across the table, Harold would see not his date's smiling, Botox-smooth face but—Eleanor's! There she was, a mean shimmering specter: stoop-shouldered over her plate, dour, pink-cheeked, shit-brown eyes squinting at him from behind horn-rimmed glasses.

His ex's trembling spectral form would open her pill case and pop a stunning assortment of vitamins, amino acids, herbal supplements, and the like. How could he not flash back to all those waiters staring at his health-obsessed wife? *Even worse.* Come evenings, when Harold and this same smooth-faced date would take off their shoes on his couch in front of the TV set, getting cozy as he flipped channels with the remote, he'd stiffen and picture the romantic evening's polar opposite: his wife gaping with disgust at the sight of Harold's fungus-mottled toenails (an old man's disease!), goading him to shame and anger. "Jeez, Harry. Have you been pressing grapes with your feet again?"

Harold switched off the ignition, his ex-wife's old taunt echoing hurtfully in his head. Swallowing his residual rage and grief, he pocketed the Mustang key. After all, since the divorce he'd licked the unsightly foot fungus with medication, and his toenails now nearly gleamed, clear as day. Sure, he still felt self-conscious on some level about shucking his socks in front of someone new. But a poem written by his Danny in first or second grade (a copy of which he'd stuck on his refrigerator door) gave Harold comfort: *Days pass! Nights too! Every day is something new!*

Even sons get second chances, Harold figured. Feet, too. Buoyed by the thought, Harold turned to his passenger and broke their long awkward silence. "Anyway we're finally here. 'Days pass, nights too. Every day's something new!' Remember that poem? I put a copy on the Frigidaire."

"Frigidaire?"

"Mine. To remind me every day's something new! Because this weekend will be a new leaf. For both of us."

"I wrote the poem?"

"How the hell can you not remember it?" Harold tsked and went out and checked in at the office and flirted with the young female clerk.

Then father and son dragged their suitcases from the back of the Mustang and rolled them across a cracked asphalt path to their King Mensch Suite, its two queen-sized beds made up tight enough to bounce a quarter on. Eager to get settled, Harold unpacked his suitcase and neatly stacked his clothes in dresser drawers. Danny, however, just sat on his unpacked suitcase staring at the noisy pyrotechnics on MTV.

"Everything's going to go great, so relax," Harold said, turning down the TV volume. "Just remember the code. If you find a sock tied to the outside doorknob, you sleep in the car. Got it? Of course, it works both ways. By the way, you got any clean socks you can spare?"

"Er, why you talking about socks?"

"Doorknob. We hang a sock on the doorknob of the room if one of us gets lucky. A trick I learned in college. What's wrong, you don't think an old fart can get lucky?"

Harold tossed Danny one of his socks.

Chapter Six

TWO HOURS LATER, HAROLD LED HIS SON ACROSS a soggy bocce field to a 70s-style dance hall, its faded peeling pink façade festooned with blinking Christmas lights (in April, no less) and a glittering gold banner announcing "The Disco Ball." The two stepped inside the sparkle-walled ballroom, its high violet ceilings strung with gaudy chandeliers, spirochete ribbons, and, for some reason, a couple of piñatas shaped like blowfish. Hanging from a central chandelier was a vintage 1970s disco ball shooting bullets of light in all directions like a sniper on steroids.

Harold brought him to the Jewish-style smorgasbord, but at the last minute his son veered to the open bar. They met again near the dance floor, at the cocktail table where Harold sat.

Clutching four splashing drinks, Danny placed the vodka and tonics on the table and wrinkled his nose at Harold's overflowing plate of brisket, spring rolls, pigs-in-blankets, and the like.

"Check out the disco ball—a genuine 1970s relic!" Harold said, bubbling over like a kid in a candy shop.

"Guess it's why they call this the Disco Ball," his son said in a world-weary way, polishing off a second drink. Harold sharply eyed him, prompting Danny to add, "Dad, it's not like

I have cancer of the liver. Besides, these drinks are so watery you need at least six to feel like you've had one."

"Well, I thought one of these drinks was for me. Meanwhile feel free to steal one of my pigs-in-a-blanket."

Danny slid one of the drinks to his father but didn't reach for food. Instead he crunched on an ice cube. Harold noticed him gripping his glass tighter, knuckles whitening, as he glanced around the room at female prospects teetering in heels.

"It's going to be like flies to shit, kid," Harold said. "For both of us. Know why? First, there's more of them than there is of us. How many men do you see around here? Fact is, we're part of a dying breed. We're keeling over every day from heart attacks, rectal cancer … there's hardly any of us left! But women—they're survivors."

"You must feel pretty lucky other men are dying."

"We both are, kid," Harold said hopefully. "You with the cancer. Me with old age."

When his son didn't reply, Harold stood to refill his plate and returned, ten minutes later, plate piled anew with pigs-in-blankets, Hawaiian chicken, and Swedish meatballs. "I might have to move around my shuffleboard schedule a bit," he told his son. "But maybe I'll stand my ground!"

Danny peered up from behind a lengthening row of empty drink glasses. "Whad'you talking about?"

"For some reason Long Island chickadees seem to collect at the salad bar. Four phone numbers so far! Hey!" Harold pointed to a well-preserved, dark-skinned woman in a short skirt standing alone at the edge of the dance floor, evidently the only female in the place south of forty-five. "Ooh-la-la. Do you see what I see?"

His son squinted at her. "Nose pin. Set in silver. Hmmm. Looks like she took a wrong turn at the Taj Mahal."

"This is your calling card," Harold said. "You each use nose metal. She doesn't even appear Jewish. I mean, what the hell did Jewish do for you the first time around?"

The disco staple "Stayin' Alive" came on, prompting his son to comment, "An appropriate standard around here."

But after "Stayin' Alive," Michael Jackson's "Beat It" took over the room. Danny scratched his head in indecision, revealing dark patches of sweat under his arms. He stood. Walking unsteadily to the dark-skinned woman, he touched her arm and then, Harold saw, led her to the dance floor.

Maybe there's hope for the poor schmuck, Harold thought—when a voice jerked his attention.

"Harry? Is it really you? It's been too long!"

Mona, a tall gray-haired number with sparkling blue eyes, stood before Harold in a tight-fitting golden dress. Talk about coincidences! The mother of Danny's best friend Steve! Like Harold, she'd divorced at a late age. He'd first met her in this exact same place and event, three years earlier. Though they'd gone out on a couple of dates back in Brooklyn, they'd since drifted.

"Mona, you sure look good. You'd better sit or else!"

As they caught up over drinks, the Village People's "Macho Man" came on, and Harold sensed the old energy surging through his feet. Pulling Mona to the dance floor, he did his lefts, rights, something he referred to as the "Lox Trot." Mona's eyes smiled, making him feel like Fred Astaire to her Ginger Rogers, as he dipped her low (ignoring the soreness in his lower back), the frosted tips of her hair tickling the skin of his right arm. She crowned him king of a realm where memories of his ex-wife couldn't put the kabosh on him.

The dance floor grew crowded. So engaged was Harold as his four limbs flailed this way and that, he lost sight of his son. He was probably chatting it up with the immigrant chick in some corner, so why fret?

After "Macho Man," Harold and Mona returned to the table and nursed Tom Collins. Harold left for refills, but on his third trip returned with news: the bar stopped selling at 10 p.m. "Come back to my room for a drink from the mini-bar, what do you say?"

Mona's eyes darted playfully left and right as if Harold were addressing someone other than she. Then she pointed to herself, silently mouthing the word: "Moi?"

"Oui! Oui!"

"Are we in a movie or something, honey?" she asked. "Casablanca?"

"If we are, let's skip the scene where you slap me in the face."

"Dream on, mister." Laughing, she stood and took his bent elbow. They left the hall. It had begun to rain outside, a steady drizzle. "Maybe we should take a water taxi," she joked squishing alongside him in the dark. "Don't you have those in Coney Island?"

"No, but we have sand fleas," he joked. Halfway there one of Mona's high heels became stuck in the mud; Harold gave her a lop-sided smile like Indiana Jones, grabbed her waist, and pulled her to drier land.

"My hero!" she gushed.

Dripping their way down the hallway, they finally came to Harold's room.

There was a sock hanging from the doorknob.

"Crap," Harold said.

"Is it yours?"

"Yeah. But I didn't put it there."

"I see," she said politely, evidently not seeing. "Do you have the key? You promised me another drink, Harold Plotnick."

"We can't go in. Like I said, I'm with my son this weekend. This here sock means he wants his privacy. If you know what I mean. Why don't we go back to your place?"

"Can't. My girlfriend who's sharing the room with me already turned in. But—wait a minute. Who needs a key?"

Mona touched the door, and it opened.

Harold's shirtless son sat by a window in the room wearing headphones. His head nodded spastically; his bare torso gleamed pale and freckled in the half light; the scar from his operation grimaced across his lower neck. Empty mini-bar bottles lined the table where he sat.

Danny raised his eyes. "Where the hell Steve's mother come from?" he said, thickly.

"Hey, Danny," Mona called over from the doorway. "So nice to see you too!"

Harold took the headphones off his son's head. "Never mind where she came from," he said. "You go to the car for a while. Here's the key to my Mustang. Go run the motor if you want. The heat works good. I'll flick the bathroom light twice in a row to let you know you can come back. And put on your shirt. Got it?"

"No way I'm sleeping in the car," he said, as he put the headphones back on.

"Yoo hoo!" Mona called. "You two okay?"

"No way I'm sleeping in the damn car," Danny repeated, louder.

Mona came over and placed her hand on Harold's shoulder. "Why don't I see you over breakfast? I hear the jelly donuts are to die for. Lend me an umbrella, Harry?"

"Wait. Don't go."

Mona squeezed his arm. "Your son seems like a nice guy. A little gothic but nice. In fact I'm glad he's my son's best friend. But he's clearly having a bad night. Just give me your umbrella, Harry. Take care of your boy, and call me in the morning."

As soon as Mona shut the door behind her, Harold lifted both earphones off his son's head and held them well out of reach.

"Don't even say you're sorry. Don't bother. It's enough you're rude to my date on a weekend I paid for. You're drunk and listening to suicidal music. You hung a sock out without reason. You're violating every rule in my book, and I have a lot of rules."

Danny reached for his pajamas. "Tired of dates. Yours … and mine."

"Don't you think it's time you moved on from your crap!" Harold snapped. "I was married for thirty-five years. You—a year. I suffered thirty-five times more than you did. And I'm *fine.*"

"Who the f cares if you're fine."

"F?" Harold slammed the headphones on the table.

Danny picked up the headset. The cord was snapped in two. He ejected his heavy-metal CD from his Discman and replaced it in its case. For a moment he stared at the cover—a group of men with long, dark hair and pale skin and black clothes, milling about like they were taking a break from the set of a Dracula movie.

"Yeah you and Mom were married like forever, and see what happened?" he said. "And sometimes it's easier to write a long letter than a short letter."

"That's why you came here this weekend, right? You came to write a longer letter. Don't you see? To make the short letter longer. But then you go ahead and mess things up with that Indian woman you danced with. Er, how did you mess up anyway?"

Danny told his father. After dancing several numbers with the woman—Danny gracelessly gothic, she doing some *I Dream of Jeannie* thing—they struggled for conversation over drinks. And more drinks. Danny said he felt surprised the woman agreed to go back with him to the room. They sat on the bed and talked. In a burst of drunken honesty, Danny told her all about his cancer, and divorce, right down to his wife's unseemly weight gain.

"This is where I went wrong," Danny went on, shaking his head. "Turns out this chick, Vinitra, is studying to be a pediatrician. I had fantasies of her giving me a thorough examination. But I was wrong about her. I figured piercings in out-of-the-way places wouldn't freak out a doctor. But after I put out your sock, and she saw my you-know-what … then she…"

"Your you-know-what?"

"Exactly. My you-know-what. And when she saw my pierced you-know-what, you know what Vinitra did?"

"No. What?"

"She tucked her shirt back in and didn't want to get involved. She mentioned her 'boyfriend in the city.' And then she walked out. I figured I'd keep the sock hanging there in the hallway as a kind of public memorial to sexual cynicism."

"You have a ring on your penis?" Harold asked.

"It's not a ring. It's a stud."

"You … gothic weirdo. Listen, from now on you're on your own, kid. Pick up the pieces of your own life!" Filled with disgust, Harold went to the bathroom and slammed the door.

Morning arrived without further incident. Harold left his son sipping black coffee in the dining hall and went to exchange contact information with Mona, splitting a jelly donut with her. Returning to their room, father and son packed up without a word between them.

Harold experienced last-minute remorse for disconnecting from his son. As they both settled in the front seat of the Mustang he saw, through the windshield, about thirty yards away, a great chapel oak in ruins, its head shattered by a thunderbolt from a recent storm. He stared at it for a moment, his head aching with something similar: survivor's guilt. As if he'd witnessed a terrible crime and did nothing to stop it. The murder of his son's normality.

Then the moment of remorse fled. Harold switched on the ignition; they rode without speaking back down Route 17, the spine of the Catskills. To distract himself, Harold focused like a laparoscopic laser on his night on the dance floor with Mona: picturing and re-picturing how she twirled with glittering dress flaring up, stockings clinging to her still-shapely legs, the way she gazed at him with adoring eyes like a welcome committee. *How come I lost touch with her for so long? She has great eyes.* And, finally, how she smelled and felt— whispering of lemons and pineapples, of cushy beach towels and lounge chairs, a nice mid-afternoon snooze, sun setting like a flesh-colored peach over blue ocean as in one of those TV commercials for Jamaica.

Just as they exited Route 17 for the Thruway south the darkish sky opened up again but briefly, then cleared long enough to fill the southern horizon with gauzy haze. Harold drove his usual fifty-five in a sixty-five; cars whizzed past on both sides, spraying the windshield with dirty specks. Returning weekend traffic built by lunchtime. He inserted his Village People into the car music player: "I wanna be—a macho man!" He sang and slapped the steering wheel to the beat, struggling to drown out his weakness for the broken kid next to him, who was fidgeting with broken headphones and shrinking into the seat.

The "Macho Man" hit screamed above the Hudson Valley, at one point scaring a bunch of starlings from a tree, scattering them like black peas. At another point, after the sky cleared enough for Harold to open the top, a shiny black Monte Carlo in the next lane edged up alongside and kept pace: its driver, also playing disco music, slicked back his hair with his hand and mistakenly gave Danny, not his father, the brotherly thumb's up. Harold adjusted the stereo volume higher.

They came to the New York City limits: a digital roadside sign warned of construction work up ahead on the George Washington Bridge. Traffic slowed; Harold furrowed his brows with concern. Shortly after the tollbooths, midway across the bridge, construction forced the Mustang and the other traffic to a complete halt.

"Goddamnit!" Harold yelled above his Village People music. "Always happens at the GW. Giuliani is fixing this bridge since he got into office…"

He unfurled a road atlas and glared at its incomprehensible web of roads for an alternative. When all of a sudden, while he was distracted, his "Macho Man" music stopped, courtesy of his son—and Six Dead Bolts assaulted the air:

Got nothing in common, him and me
He blames me for his injury
He wants to help but only hurts,
Locks me in his custody.

He makes me dance with the grim reaper's wife
But I ain't done yet with this fool life
Got death in my bones like a bad disease—
I die each time he stares at me.

"So your car *does* play CDs!" his son shouted above the noise.

Harold was stunned as the so-called music screeched above the roadway, between the steel cables, making them nearly tremble. Finally he slammed his fist against the steering wheel. He reached across the seat. In one indignant motion he managed to eject the CD and re-insert his "Macho Man" tape—his other hand holding Six Dead Bolts out of reach from his son.

Macho macho man!

As disco pounded anew, his son tried to grab his heavy metal CD back: with red faces and impassioned grunts, both Plotnicks wrestled in the front seat, tugging the CD toward opposite sides of the idling car.

All at once the CD loosed from their grips, shooting into the air. It whizzed through the Mustang's open roof. As they watched with mouths agape, it sailed south like a Frisbee over three lanes of cars, weaving through space between steel cables, lofting toward the edge. It touched down, oddly enough, on the flat upper rail of the bridge's perimeter fence—presumably with a clear view of the Hudson River.

Harold was paralyzed as his kid, without a word, opened the Mustang door and stepped out. He strode between stalled honking cars and trucks, crossing three lanes, a man on a mission.

Hands grasping the perimeter fence, elbows locking into ninety-degree angles, Danny vaulted over to the other side, where he landed on a lip of bridge jutting out over the far-below river.

Harold snapped to attention. He climbed out of the Mustang with such haste he left the door open. He cursed at the cursing drivers and honking vehicles as he headed for the edge of the bridge.

Harold approached the perimeter fence and saw his son standing on the other side a few feet away, clasping a steel cable—and, beyond his skinny form, the distant river glinting in the windy afternoon like shattered safety glass.

Harold's palms broke out in sweat, his throat went dry, his heart beat so hard he felt it through his chest. "Don't!" he shouted, thinking of the impact—the boy's body going from eighty mph to nearly zero in a nanosecond. Ribs getting shoved into heart and lungs. The physics of inertia being what they are, internal organs tend to keep going.

"Oh, hi," his son said through the fence in a shaky voice. "I'm a tad busy right now." He tightened his grip on the cable. With the other hand he reached for the CD, which lay on the fence post a few feet from where he stood.

As Danny inched forward, Harold, fearing the worst, flailed desperately through the fence to try to grab him. He succeeded in clasping a shirt sleeve. "*Shit!*" Danny muttered, thrown off balance by his father's attempt.

Danny managed to regain his footing—but knocked the CD off the post.

The disc wobbled down through empty space, sending up brief bullets of light through the fence.

Harold yelled, "You were trying to get your CD back, right? You're not jumping?"

"Does it matter?"

"It does matter. I'll buy you a new CD. How much could Five Dead Bolts cost?"

"*Six* Dead Bolts!"

"Don't play dumb with me mister. Just grab my hand. I mean, whatever have you done for me? Except maybe you gave me an ulcer."

"I guess you're expressing how much you care."

"I do care! You're why I suffered with your mother for thirty-five years," Harold said. "I did it for you, Danny. I wanted you to have a real family. I didn't want you to grow up dysfunctional."

"I guess your strategy didn't work." Danny again regarded the river. His hand clasped and unclasped the steel cable as if considering something.

Harold's eyes widened. His hand jerked through the fence and came out the other side, flailing even more wildly for his son.

Harold's fingers snapped around the shirt collar; his son coughed as the shirt pulled tight around his neck and tried to wrench himself free.

He did—but lost his balance again, feet doing a little shuffle-step on the ledge. Harold saw his son's face jerk upward, gazing at the clouds, and followed his line of sight. Seagulls wheeled down on great white wings—a police helicopter shifted sideways, blades slicing empty space like scalpels tossed by a cosmic surgeon.

Danny went down.

Chapter Seven

ATTACHED TO A WOODEN POLE TWO STORIES above Queens Boulevard, Steve Kirsch was speaking emphatically into his cell phone—"return my goddamn pants already!"—when another call beeped him. Checking the caller ID, he rapped his fed-up knuckles against his hard hat. Literally up a pole most days, he didn't appreciate casual calls during work, particularly two at the same time. Both from women who made him feel tense.

Steve needed to stay calm and focused when making communications decisions that could affect chunks of New York City. Thousands of calls, Steve liked to think, could be affected by a slip of his wire splicer. Not to mention the risk getting distracted could cause Steve to lose his footing and plunge through the roof of some passing car, becoming the lead item on the five o'clock news.

"Gotta go," he said, to the first caller. "Just mail me my pants, as I already mentioned. What? Sure, I have an extra pair. I'm wearing them! But all my uniforms are property of Bell Atlantic so you, my dear, are flirting with larceny. Anyway, this conversation is officially over. Why? My mother's on the other line, that's why. What? Jesus, you sound jealous. I mean, it's like you're jealous of my *mother*. Like you even have a right to be jealous." He pressed end and shook his head. "Chicks," he muttered, pressing flash.

"Sorry to keep you waiting, Mom," he said. "It was only my thieving ex-girlfriend on the other line."

"My God, how did you know it was me?" Mona said through the phone.

"About twenty-five years ago, they came out with something named caller ID. A big leap forward at the time. In fact, I honored you by actually picking up the phone and not letting it go to voicemail. You know, honor thy—"

"Enough of your meshugas! This is important Steve. Are you sitting down?"

"Can't, uh, sit down right now. You might say I'm a bit up in the air with my job."

"You should think of going back to law school, Stevie. Instead of wasting away at your dead-end job waiting around for a pink slip!"

"No. I mean, I'm up a pole fixing stuff. There's zero place to sit. This is not about layoffs. I'm not up in the air *about* my job. In a non-physical sense, at least, my job is safe. Anyhow, Mom, what's up? I mean, why did you call me at work? I hate calls at work."

"You're telling me physically your work is unsafe?" she yelled into Steve's left ear. "This is supposed to reassure me? That's all I need. Another kid…" Mona's sniffle came clearly through the phone. "Don't lie to me. Do you or do you not have a good grip on whatever it is you keep a grip on?"

"I'm holding onto the line receptor box. I'm hooked to the pole," he said, playing the good son. "Go ahead."

"Good. Don't let go. Remember: good grip. You work like a circus acrobat, clinging to the side of Mount Everest. Anyway, I need to tell you about Dan, your friend, the one who re-introduced me to his father Harold, thank God."

"He did?"

"This past weekend. Remember I told you I was going up to the Catskills on a singles weekend? Anyway, that's besides the point."

"What *is* the point?"

"Danny went off the GW Bridge and..." Mona's voice broke. "It's like an earthquake hit Harold! He feels responsible. Of course, *he's* the father, but *I* don't know what to do."

Steve stared down with confusion at the little cars driving past. "You're saying what?"

"Jumped, pushed, what's the difference. Everything's still being sorted out. Just a few hours ago it happened. Harry was there—can you believe he was there?"

"No. No, I can't." Steve spoke woodenly.

"But here's the thing," Mona said. "He's okay now."

"Harold is?"

"Not Harry. Harry is not fine. Like I said, he feels personally responsible for this meshugas. He's a mess of emotions! I mean *Dan* is fine. Bruised, of course, and the doctor says he may have a nose scar for the rest of his life, and he's in a thick fog, can hardly remember who he is, hardly recognizes his own father, doesn't even want to see him, but other than this, he's resting quietly in the hospital."

Steve relaxed his grip on the receptor box. "Dan isn't dead?"

"Right. It's not like he's dead or anything."

"He's not *like* dead? You mean, he's brain dead?"

"No. He's definitely not dead. Though he hardly talks to anyone. But that's probably his personality anyway."

Steve said nothing.

"You okay?" she asked.

"Yeah," Steve replied weakly. "Just tell me one thing. How come he's not dead? He went off the GW Bridge, didn't he?"

"Dan was saved by a construction net—a miracle!"

Feeling quiet inside, Steve sat down.

"Oh, Stevie, I hear a horrible creaking. You're not sitting down on that shaky platform? You told me you shouldn't sit."

"Sorry, I figured out how. There's a two-inch wide flat surface on the rail of this cage contraption I'm in."

"My God. Don't stay there too long. You're obese. You're a hundred feet in the air!"

"I'm overweight. Obese is a whole different ballgame. And I'm thirty-five feet in the air. And after the roller-coaster hell you just put me through, I need to sit. He's dead! Brain-dead! Not dead! Jeez." Steve gave a nervous little laugh. "What hospital's he at anyway?"

"Columbia-Presbyterian. He's under observation. *Stand up right now.* All I need is two kids in one day plunging from a high place."

"Observation?"

"Well, you know, he tried to leave this world. And now I'm afraid for *you* honey."

"It's not like he succeeded or anything."

"He didn't succeed or anything, so it doesn't matter?"

"Of course it matters, Mom, and don't distort what I say. Anyway, I need to get off the phone. I'm punching out early to see Dan."

"Here's the thing. His father and I need to talk to you. In person. Before you go visit. This is why I'm calling you. You need to come over to my place this minute. Harry's here right now. But first *promise me promise me* you'll stand up!"

Steve hung up the phone and creakily stood. Below him, traffic seethed impatiently. An eighteen-wheeler bellowed black smoke from its twin chrome exhaust pipes like a furiously snorting bull. For a long time Steve stared down at the cars and trucks. It occurred to him he'd forgotten to ask his mother why he had to see her first. This was how flummoxed he felt.

Chapter Eight

SEVERAL HOURS BEFORE STEVE FOUND OUT, Daniel Plotnick had regained consciousness, battered and bruised. At first, he didn't know where he was. He seemed to be lying in a hospital bed, a bandage covering his nose. Sure, his face ached with hazy recollections of being blown flat by a wall of wind that nebulized his eyes, curled back his lips, cauterized his gums, and stuffed a curdling scream back down his throat— as primal pain stun-gunned his nose. Then: a white nothingness. But beyond these sensations, he didn't know much. He felt incredibly sore. Disgusted. Confused as to why he wasn't dead.

To distract himself from the doom he dimly felt, he took to counting the drips from his IV bag. Around the seventy-fifth, a doctor came into his room. Dr. Ahmed unclipped a pen-sized flashlight from his pocket, and said, "Mr. Plotnick, you will see a brightness, but only for a moment." He aimed the light in his eyes, and so he experienced a blinding light, and a hopeful expression passed over the doctor's face.

A second medical professional, prim red-haired woman with an ID card clipped to her blouse, pulled up a chair. Dr. Katar was a staff psychologist. "Dr. Ahmed asked me to join him. Do you mind some questions? Good. Your father wants to pop in but we feel it would be best for him to wait. We'd like you to lie quietly for now."

"My ... father." He tried to smile but a pang of pain in his face stopped him short. "Too noisy, right?"

The doctors exchanged a glance. Being vague came more easily to him than remembering. And as Dr. Katar continued asking, probing this and that cob-webbed corner of his brain, there was something painful attached to this remembering business. So they fleshed out details for him, about his nose ring catching on a protrusion on the way down, about how sorry his father was for accidentally pushing him off, things like that, and after a while he felt he'd rather let it rest, and told them so.

This was a lot of information to process, though, and Plotnick managed to lean up in bed and call back the doctor before she left the room. "Er, one more question…"

Dr. Katar turned the lights back on and stuck her head back in. "Yes, Mr. Plotnick?"

"How come … I'm not dead?"

The doctor let out an embarrassed heart-felt sigh. "Of course. Sorry for leaving out that part. How can I put this?" She smiled. "Did you vote for Mayor Giuliani in the last election?"

"I honestly don't remember."

"You should have. All that money he wasted? He's six hundred million over budget on bridge repair."

"Er…"

"You, my good sir, fell into a construction net. The police said you couldn't have fallen more than twenty-five feet. You practically fell into a trampoline. You're lucky to be alive," she said. "A very good use of our bridge toll money, I might add."

"Funny," he said, as she turned to go.

"What?"

"You know. Cost overruns and that sort of thing. Should be bad, not good. Unfinished repairs. Should be a negative, not a positive." He tried to chuckle but grimaced instead. "You know. It's the opposite of what you expect."

Opposite. He let the word play across the surface of his brain.

"Very interesting, Mr. Plotnick. Now get some rest. We'll see you in the morning and continue probing your memory. Sound like a plan?"

Dr. Katar lowered the lights a last time, said good day, and disappeared into the shadows of the hallway.

Just as the door clicked shut, something clicked in his brain.

The past twelve months came rushing back to him. Painfully precise. Cataclysmically clear. *Twenty-five feet my ass*, he thought, recalling in detail the lousiest day, and year, of his life.

He felt he'd plunged all the way to the Hudson River.

His fingers wandered across the eight-inch scar etched into his lower neck like a bas-relief grin. The dermal hieroglyphics told a story. His story. A story rivaling the descent of Job, whose catastrophic loss of family, fortune, and faith in God took up only a chapter in the Bible. Also, the Ten Plagues of Egypt. The wisdom of it. How cramming all those locusts and frogs and death into a short time got the suffering over and done with. A potential bright side, when you really thought about it.

The only thing that saved Plotnick from his own breath-taking plunge was contrary to what you'd expect.

While the opposite concept was not new to him, never before had it resounded so emphatically, as he lay in a hospital bed, lucky to have survived at all.

He resolved to go when the proverbial light was red. Stop on green. Eat chocolate ice cream when he craved vanilla. Choose a woman not at all like his ex-wife. Never go to the Catskills again—or talk with his father.

That's what he needed to do, he mused.

Steve buzzed his mother's apartment: the door immediately swung open. Harold Plotnick stood there ashen and grim-faced as if he'd been glued for hours to this very spot waiting for Steve to arrive.

"Thank God you're here," Harold said, extending his hand.

"Funny seeing you at my mom's, Mr. P," Steve said, returning the shake. "How come you're not in the hospital with Danny?"

Harold wrung his hands and gestured for Steve to follow him into the next room, where Mona sat on her living room couch next to a box of tissues. He directed Steve to sit across from her, and sat to the left of Mona on the other side of the box, as if he'd carefully choreographed the scene in advance.

Harold clasped Steve's right shoulder. He stared at him even as he asked Mona, "Think your kid's up for this?"

"What kind of question is this? Of course. He's my son."

Steve impatiently checked his watch. He wanted to make visiting hours. "Er, Mr. P. . . . ?"

"Please call me Harold. I know you're in a rush so I'll get right to it. Here's what I have to say. Without any more banter or beating around the bush. I've known you, Steve, for a while and you've been a friend to my son. A *good* friend. But choosing a proxy is one of the most important choices I'll ever make. Second only to divorcing my son's mother."

"I don't catch your drift, Mr. P."

"I need help reaching out to Danny. Because it's not merely that my son went off the side of you-know-what and I feel responsible even though he didn't get hurt too much and this in itself is a miracle. It's because, so help me, I feel I don't have a son."

"No?"

"He won't let me in the hospital room. He doesn't give me time of day. I called him earlier and he didn't want to talk, which I told him was a 'real slap.' He hung up anyway. But why wouldn't he? First I didn't show up to his marital lockout and then I took him to the Catskills to old-lady land and then I literally drove him to the brink. Just my being in the hospital with him another minute'd make him jump out the window from another high place." He was red-faced, trembling. "I'm no good for him. I can't help him anymore. But…"

Mona placed a comforting hand on Harold's cheek.

"Why don't you tell him everything, Harry?"

"Sit down, Steve," Harold said.

"I am sitting," Steve said, and so Harold told the story.

"Jeez, you pushed him?" Steve said a few minutes later.

"Not what I said!" Harold said, his face twisted and mottled. "I tried to grab him but I'm a clutz, okay? My whole life I've been a clutz! Never more so than when I took my only child to the Catskills."

"Just tell me one more thing," Steve said. "What are you doing here with my mother? You rekindled your romance this past weekend?"

"That's right, Stevie!" Mona said, breaking her silence. She took Harold's hand. "This whole Catskills experience drew us closer. This experiment in mortality has made us like fellow scientists on the brink of some terrible discovery."

"You're all I've got, Steve." Harold's voice cracked. "You gotta help me be a father to him. I could literally list the ways to help fix his life. In fact, I have."

"Again, I'm not following."

"Don't you get it? The newspapers are all over this! A *New York Post* reporter called already. By his questions, I can already see the headline: Bridge Jumper Driven to Despair by his Father's Musical Tastes. You see, I … and then he … he …"

Again, the voice petered out.

"I played disco but he wanted heavy metal!" Harold blurted out.

"Sheesh. The 'Macho Man' shit you like? How long did you play it?"

"The whole ride down. Right up until the bridge. I knew he wanted to hear his construction noise music. But did I care? No! I wanted to enjoy my 'Macho Man.' To feel like I was back on the dance floor."

"With me," Mona said, with a sad smile.

"With you," Harold said, eyes glistening. "But the disco made Danny feel bad, I know it. It reminded him how he met the Pakistani chick who stole his heart. 'Cause he met her on the dance floor, to the beat of 'Macho Man'!"

"Jeez." Steve placed a firm hand on Harold's shoulder. "I got it, Mr. P. Your son hated disco as much as you loved it. Okay," he said. "I'm already regretting this, but I'll agree to whatever it is you want me to do. Can't be too difficult, right?" Steve tentatively patted the elderly Plotnick on the back.

"Honestly, it won't be a cake walk," Harold said. "I mean, we're down to brass tacks here—how to fix a weirdo kid broken inside and out."

Mona unfolded a piece of paper with formatted instructions.

"You typed it?" Steve said.

"Mona did. I dictated."

"Onto an Excel spreadsheet?"

Mona smiled. "Everyone needs a good secretary."

Steve read out loud. "Item one. Change clothes from black to normal. Item three. Go back to work. Four. Get decent girlfriend. Five. Change musical tastes to something less suicidal. Six. Take a vacation if you can afford it, maybe to Mexico. I hear Cancun is cheap. Seven. Get plenty of exercise and sunshine. Eight…" Steve paused, glancing up. "Just one question, Mr. P."

"Call me Harold."

"Harold. Why did you cross out item two, 'Lose nose ring'?"

"He … and then…"

Harold's voice trailed off.

"It's okay, Mr. P. I'll figure it out on my own."

Steve was a union man. A team player. But still…

"So all these items are things you want him to do?"

"Correct."

"And you expect me to get him to do them?"

"Of course, feel free to play with the order of these items. Use your judgment." Harold smiled. "The important thing is you're my proxy. You'll report back to me. We'll set up a reporting system. I've already taken the online tutorial for Microsoft Excel."

Mona touched her forehead, indicating the mind. "Stevie-Pie. Harold's a retired CPA, as you very much know. He can do your income taxes forever if you need."

"Forever? Jeez. I'm only trying to get through today."

"I know someday he'll talk to me again," Harold said, handing Steve the spreadsheet. "I think I'd like that."

Steve rechecked his watch and stiffly stood, the task before him already weighing on his meaty shoulders. For most of his adult life he'd taken pride knowing the answer to complex situations, at least when it came to phones. All he needed were the right tools and attitude. His connections, literally—his power to make or break when and to whom people connected—radiated out into all his affairs. Pity the telemarketer who pitched Steve at home: he might find his service mysteriously cut off. God save those proselytizing Jehovah's witnesses who rang his bell at dinnertime: next day they were paying customers of Psychic Hotline.

But fixing a broken buddy on behalf of his distraught father was an entirely different matter.

"I'll email you how it goes," Steve told Harold at the door.

Steve caught a subway into Manhattan, managing to arrive at Columbia-Presbyterian before the end of visiting hours. But when Steve found the floor nurse, she informed him Daniel Plotnick was refusing to see any visitors. No exceptions.

"You're a schmuck, Plotnick," Steve muttered to himself in the hallway. Then he resignedly headed home.

For Steve Kirsch, it had been a very, very long day.

A few days later, Dr. Katar jotted "Memory Recovered" in Daniel Plotnick's chart, a nurse popped out his intravenous tube and, finally, a medical resident snipped the stitches, revealing a scar across one nostril far smaller and less obvious—Plotnick observed in the mirror with no small relief—than the eight-inch one marring his neck.

The hospital released him to his own devices and he took the subway back to his bachelor pad in Brooklyn. Unlocking the door for the first time in a week, Plotnick stood for a moment staring in. The apartment was half empty. Only a desk and chair in a corner of the living room. Plotnick hadn't refurnished his space since evicting his ex.

In the weeks immediately following the police showdown Judy had come back to pick up her belongings. They'd divided furniture; she'd taken the love seat. He discarded what neither of them wanted. He ripped down the pink-and-white striped curtains, balled the mauve bathroom rug so it fit in the garbage, poured boiling water into the bonsai plant making its leaves turn pale and taut, fed her wall posters of John Denver and James Taylor to the shredder. He covered bald patches of wall with his own posters: heavy metal musicians manhandling their guitars, striding across foggy opaque stages like ghosts haunting a London cemetery. He even cleared her browser history from the PC.

Now crossing the living room, he could hear the echo of his steps against the wooden floor. *I've been away a little while but something's different.* He went room to room. He observed a fresh water stain in the shower ceiling, and in fact a crack in the living room wall had widened a few millimeters. He checked some more. Kicking some dirty clothes here and there, his foot sent up a mildewy aroma. He cautiously opened the hall closet and was greeted by a familiar wall of old coats trying to bust out. Search and smell and listen best he could, he couldn't find what had changed. But he nevertheless sensed it.

There was something unexpected in the air.

Knock! Knock! Knock!

It was the door. Startled, Plotnick stumbled across laundry, empty Brooklyn Lager bottles, weeks-old *New York Times* and other flotsam that had collected on the floor. He unlocked the deadbolt: Steve stood in the doorway. He wore his Bell Atlantic work uniform, per usual, ringed by a utility belt of unfamiliar tools. He didn't appear happy. What struck Plotnick most was what Steve gripped in his hand: a rolled-up sheath of papers.

"Finally he answers!" Steve said. "What the hell's the matter? He doesn't answer my phone calls or let me see him at the hospital?"

"Er…"

"Don't care for your 'sorry's. So what you plunged off the GW and nearly tore your nose off? You know how long we've been friends? Since you got your first pair of long pants. I was *there* for you. And your nose looks no worse for the wear."

"It's just … I needed to be a hermit."

"Enough with the hermit stuff already. Get rid of your hermitude." Steve, disgusted, kicked at a pile of dirty clothes. "On top of you dis-ing me, coming here is like getting stranded in a cesspool without a paddle."

Steve stepped further into the apartment and tightened the papers he held into a skinny tube, waving it in the air like a professorial wand. He cried out, "Ahem! Welcome to the Ripley's Believe-It-Or-Not tour of your apartment. Also known as the Daniel E. Plotnick memorial garbage dump."

He swept the roll of papers through the air and pointed to grease stains on the kitchen wall. "Mess!"

He pointed out a dead plant in a pot on the window sill. "Mess! And finally, ladies and gents..."

With dramatic flourish, Steve kicked up a pair of dirty socks from the floor, deftly causing one to arc through the air and land on Plotnick's head. "Mess!"

"Stop pointing that freakin' thing." Plotnick brushed the sock from his head and snatched the roll of papers from Steve, unrolling it. He examined the papers with irritated interest. "What is this, some sort of *list*?"

Plotnick read his father's suggested lifestyle changes to himself. "Just one question. What's number two about?" he said, pointing to a scribbled over item. He looked closer and touched his nose. "Lose ... nose ... ring. I see! So Steve, let me take a wild guess. This to-do list, or whatever, comes from my father?"

"Er, what makes you think that?"

"It's got his fingerprints all over it."

Steve nodded. "He figures you'll never talk to him again, but me, well, me and you go way back."

"You're his *proxy*?"

"In fact, that's the word he used. It's his way of showing he cares." Steve tugged up his pants and tightened his utility belt.

"So he wants me to do these things?" Plotnick said.

"Correcto mundo."

"And he expects you to get me to do them?"

"Of course, as your father says, feel free to play with the order of these items. Use your judgment." Steve smiled encouragingly.

"You know, I'd bust out laughing if my face didn't hurt so much. But maybe I will anyway." Plotnick let out a half-hearted chuckle. "Hah! Ow!"

"Another thing." Steve handed Plotnick a second sheet of paper. "Here's my own list. Kinda expands on your father's number four suggestion."

"Number four?" Plotnick skimmed the page. "Jennifer Defazio. Emma Fitzpatrick. Deb Juno? And what's this part? 'Speak English and cute. Live legally in the United States. None are senior citizens or ex-convicts.'"

Plotnick squinted with suspicion at Steve. "Who are these women? What's going on here?"

"Calm, bro. They're sisters and an ex-wife of Bell Atlantic buddies. I cashed in a couple of favors for you. Your schedule is booked for the next three Friday nights out."

Plotnick rolled his eyes with exasperation. "All right, Steve, I've tolerated your presence up to now. But this is how you want to come back into my life? With *lists*? How could I ever date again? It's like I'm walking around with a big D and C across my shirt. I have yet to recover from my father shoving old bags down my throat."

"Whoa! Don't go there. You're insulting my mother, who technically could be an old bag," Steve said. "And now, by the way, she's your father's new girlfriend. So let's curb old people put-downs."

"You mean...?"

Steve nodded. "That's why there's such urgency here. There's change in the air. And it smells real bad." He warily sniffed the room. "To me it smells like rotting fruit. But the message is this: Clean your apartment. Tell the truth to people. Treat your best buddy with respect. Don't do drugs when swimming. Go out on dates. And call your father. I mean, this pathetic part of your life is over."

"Like I might call him. After the trip to the Catskills, blasting 'Macho Man,' and pushing me off the GW?"

"When you put it that way ... Ahem! Anyway, he wants to make it up to you. Here. A present from your old man." Steve handed him a gift-wrapped package.

Plotnick opened the package. It was a Metallica CD.

"He said Tower Records was all out of Five Dead Bolts," Steve explained. "Frankly, I've never heard of the group."

Plotnick didn't bother correcting the group's name. He knew one thing: he could never listen to it again. Not to lyrics that glorified dying—not after he tasted death and barely survived it. His heavy metal CD's descent into the Hudson River presaged his own terrifying plunge, minutes later. If this wasn't a sign...

"Very thoughtful of my father," he told Steve. "But you see, I'm giving up gothic. The ring, you know, nearly destroyed my face. I appreciate it, but I'm done with that crap," he said, firmly. "It's back to normal colors for me. Just the thought of heavy metal..." He handed the CD back to Steve, who reluctantly took it.

"Well, at least call your old man. He's worried sick about you after you hung up on him at the hospital. So stop being so damn angry. It doesn't make sense."

Steve tried to hand him the phone but Plotnick shook his head and gazed out the living room window at a neighboring gravel rooftop, antenna prickling the sky. Sure, it didn't make sense. But did anything? He felt drained by his father's insanity, which nearly killed him. He couldn't control the negative events in his life. But maybe he could leave behind those people who reminded him of them.

Steve sighed, placing the phone back in its cradle. "One more question from your father, before you return to being a hermit."

Plotnick answered before he even asked. "I wasn't going to jump. I slipped off the ledge. It was slippery."

"Thank you for telling me this. He thanks you. We all do. The family can now officially take you off suicide watch." He went on, "Now I'm only going to tell you this once, shithead. You want to move on from all your bad stuff. You're done with your ex-wife. Your ex-life. Time to shift to your better half. Go get yourself a chick—" Steve swept his hand through the air, re-indicating the apartment's filthiest parts. "—who knows how to freakin' clean. Time to bite the hair of the dog that bit you. And once you start dating, maybe you and your father will have something to talk about. Now wouldn't that be different?"

A bit taken aback, Plotnick scratched an eyelid thoughtfully and adjusted his glasses across his nose. The idea he'd sown in the back of his mind—to live the opposite of his former experience—gained strength, mixing with another notion: Instead of using the idea to cut items out of his life, what if he used it to add to his life?

"You got me there, Steve," he said. "It *would* be different. In fact it would be the complete opposite of my every instinct."

Chapter Nine

ON HIS DEATHBED IN A HOSPITAL IN BOGOTÁ, wounded in a car-jacking, Eduardo Cruz directed his last five words to his youngest daughter: "You are the responsible one." Then his eyes fluttered shut.

And so after he died Sonia took care of the family: her widowed mother, her two young brothers. She finished her medical degree and worked three jobs at Bogotá hospitals to make the bills. She tried to run her father's factory, which made chemical fertilizers, but it went under. She fended off creditors. She felt anything but responsible. Because being responsible meant being respected.

She didn't feel respected by her macho Colombian boyfriend, who treated her like fragile dishware—treated her to red roses and candle-lit dinners and such—but, she learned, was actually double-timing. She felt the opposite of responsible, but nonetheless grew responsible. She grew to know prayer, even while working into the wee hours as an emergency room doctor, sometimes treating criminals wounded by policemen who warned her: "Don't treat them!" She knew the value of prayer even if no longer sure God existed.

So she prayed for a U.S. student visa to solve her economic problems, received one, and flew to Florida. When she arrived she opened her purse and unpeeled a black-and-white photo that had become stuck to her Colombian national ID. It was a portrait of her father from his high school graduation. He had a pencil-thin moustache on a somber face, a head of thick boyish hair. He was younger in the photo than his daughter who now carried it.

"Am I really the responsible one?" she asked. "How can I be if I let your photo get wrinkled?" It was April 12, 1996. She traveled from Florida to New York City, crashed at her sister's apartment in New Jersey, and signed up for a Kaplan course for the U.S. medical boards. Because sometimes there's no choice. The course set her back three thousand dollars, most of her savings. This was the price and risk of making it in the United States, or so she hoped. And she sought to be a doctor in America.

It was lonely sleeping, or trying to, on her sister's couch in West Paterson, New Jersey. Her eyes stayed open until the wee hours. Gazing into the blackness of the living room ceiling she'd recall the police report that described the car-jacking. From the police description she'd picture, again and again, two darkly dressed assailants waiting for her father to leave his factory office that evening. She could imagine them pulling a gun when he refused to hand over the keys to his Mazda. Pop! Pop!

Sonia sought relief from her mind's images. Sometimes, as the first pale light of morning pinched back the blackness through the living room window, a muffled melody would come in through the glass panes. Coo-ooh! Coo-ooh! She'd sit up and peer through the window and see the pear-shaped bodies of mourning doves quivering in the vague light across the laundry line. They sang to her. The music sounded grief-stricken yet purposeful. A music that could lift her from self-pity, if she let it. The sad song plucked at her heartstrings, calmed her: her racing heartbeat slowed. Morning broke in West Paterson. Sonia managed to finally get to sleep.

Beating back old demons was no easy feat, but Sonia Cruz dug deep. When she wasn't struggling to study medical texts written in a foreign language, she strained to fill the hole in her heart by trawling the Internet for companionship, which for an immigrant woman with professional aspirations felt safer and more interesting than going to bars.

She was of deep, unabiding passion, attractive, and the photo of herself she posted on several dating sites was intriguing: a dark long-haired exotic woman straddling the ornate lip of a marble European-style fountain, a goat-demon statue spewing an arrow of water past her left shoulder. Birds smoked the cobalt blue sky. The day was windy, her mane of hair accentuating her rogue smile.

But why should an Internet-savvy immigrant attract Neanderthals instead of handsome men? Reply after reply came back with *fotos muy feas*. "Another ugly one," she said, turning away from her computer screen's image of the latest egg-shaped head, beady eyes cramping a misshapen nose, lips stretched over yellowed or crooked teeth. "Why did I ever move to the United States?"

She knew the answer: because the only thing worse than staying would be going home. She remembered this answer whenever she struggled to keep down greasy processed food, because that's all they served in the fast-food joints near the library where she studied. Even if the fruit in Colombia was the freshest and best tasting in the world—even if she went to sleep each night in New Jersey dreaming of those sweet juicy mangos, guanabanas, creamy avocadoes, and pineapples widely available in her hometown at about one-fifth the price of the hard, unripe fruit sold in New Jersey—she still needed a secure place where she could get on with her life.

She had needs too. The need to be appreciated. So she exchanged emails with the least ugly prospects, taking things to the next level. First she dated a fat manager at Sony who edited an in-house newsletter and spent his free time glued to ESPN and spoke no Spanish. Then she dated a Guatemalan handyman whose main ambition was to upgrade to a newer Dodge Ram. He spoke Spanish of such street variety even she had trouble following.

Around the time she was about to give up English because too many Americans couldn't get past her accent, and fate suggested she call it a day and go back home with nothing to show for it—a dead-end immigrant, no boyfriend, three thousand poorer—the photo of Daniel Plotnick came up. It appeared sideways on the computer screen and seemed shot during an all-male camping trip. He was unshaven, bare-chested, T-shirt in one hand, Swiss Army knife in the other. The off-kilter photo gave the impression this male prospect was falling off an edge, tumbling toward the ground. The shirt in his hand seemed swept up in a high wind, and yet Sonia could see the photo-realistic illustration across it: a buxom bikini-clad woman.

"What a loser!" she said, and couldn't help smiling at how nice this American phrase sounded.

❧   ❧

On three subsequent Fridays at the same mediocre China-town restaurant—after putting in his nine hours or so at The Associated Press—Daniel Plotnick met two sisters and an ex-wife of co-workers of Steve's, one at a time over dim sum, as if test-driving Fords across the worn and weathered rim of the Great Wall of China.

The first date Plotnick mentioned his cancer to was Jennifer DeFazio, a petite blonde with fetching blue eyes. She initially tried to comfort Plotnick, returning his despondent gaze like a young protégé of Mother Theresa. She even let him eat the last bit of dim sum. Things quickly soured, however. She phoned him the next day to cancel their weekend plans together, saying she'd enrolled in First Communion classes and planned to receive the body of Christ—presumably instead of Plotnick's—by eating wafers.

"I'm honest with every single date. They tell me they appreciate it. But none returns my calls," Plotnick said with giddy frustration, at the bar his buddy managed part-time. At 10 p.m. the place was nearly empty; Plotnick took a long pull on his beer as Steve joined him for a cold one on the customer side, clamping a meaty arm around him like a big brother.

"You have much to learn, Young Grasshopper. You should pull back. Wait until the second date to tell them your tragic life," Steve advised.

"No way. That would be lying. I think the opposite approach we agreed on is better."

"Yeah, but the truth has many shades. You don't want to send every woman except those with emotional superpowers screaming into the wilderness."

Plotnick worried his scruffy hair. "You put me up to this. You're trying to delude yourself into thinking you're helping me. And I'm playing along out of respect for our history as friends."

"Then it's time to trust me. For your own good."

"Good, shmood. If they can't face me as I really am, it's: Adios baby! I'm tired of lies." Plotnick walked to the bar's grimy window and stared out at a city bus rumbling past. "It's like taking mass transit, shopping at Staples or Office Max, Lowes or Home Depot. What's the difference? No one cares. They put umpteen million dollars into marketing, but the brand fades into meaningless jingoism. The stores are exactly the same. Fake differentiation! I for one give the American people credit to know when they've been had," Plotnick said, with a hint of sadness.

"What the hell you talking about?"

"All women are the same. Whether they're named Jennifer DeFazio or Judy Bronstein or Swift Running Water."

Steve placed a comforting paw on Plotnick's shoulder. "Let's try something else. There's a new saying going around. Over the Internet no one knows you're a dog."

"Jeez, Steve. Things are bleak, but no way I'm getting a dog. I don't want that kind of responsibility right now. I'm trying to find someone who can accept my complex and self-deprecating character."

"I'm talking about web dating, dipshit."

Plotnick thrummed his fingers impatiently on the bar. A business reporter, he knew the Internet, then in its infancy, was the Wild West of romance—everyone and his mother was in a mad dash to find a soul mate online. A guy searching for love through his computer might as well step into a dark alleyway at night. Anyone could lurk there.

"Had a better idea," he said. "I've decided to join a creative writing group. I'll share my tragic life, literally, with people who understand tragedy is art. That all lemonade starts with lemons."

"Well I think your whole idea's a lemon," Steve said, brandishing a knife he used to slice them. "And it's exactly the wrong approach. Before you go spilling the beans to strangers, give high-tech a chance. Trust me on this. With the Internet we can hide enough of your real deal to keep women from fleeing in the opposite direction."

Plotnick swigged from his beer as Steve outlined his plan. Though Plotnick was resistant, determined to join a writing group anyway, several beers later he reluctantly agreed to give it a try. The pair formed an uneasy alliance. Evenings at Plotnick's apartment, over several weeks, Steve dialed up his buddy's PC and searched singles websites. Not wanting to invest financially in what he viewed as pure folly, Plotnick selected a free but clunky dating service run by Excite.

As Steve supervised, Plotnick checked off female preferences, including the "not a big problem" box for "pleasantly plump," and "*not!*" for "happy with hefty." Several dozen women made it through this early screening process, and Steve, touting the Internet's versatility, directed Plotnick to email each of them back it would be nice to meet them.

"Got someone for you," Steve said one evening at Plotnick's apartment. "A doctor. She could have a cold mechanical view of health conditions. A possible plus for you."

"Hmm. Where's she from?"

"Latin America."

"What you crazy? Those women wear their passion inside-out. They can't hide from their emotions. She'll freak when she finds out. No way I'm replying to her."

"Too late." Plotnick watched Steve go to the computer and sit, clicking to a website. "I've been pretending to be Daniel Plotnick these last couple of weeks on my PC at home. You'd be impressed with my writing. I even uploaded your photo."

Plotnick ran over, annoyed. "I didn't give you permission!"

"My bad. But now it's time for the real Daniel Plotnick to step up to the plate."

"You stole my identity, went behind my back, and expect me to 'step up to the plate'?"

"Yeah, yeah. Cool your pits. I didn't want you to screw things up and spill the beans too fast. Here. Check out the photo she sent."

Plotnick whistled at the image on the screen. "*She's a doctor*?" The photo showed a pretty, dark-featured woman straddling the ornate lip of a marble fountain, mane of hair blowing about, smile gently lifting her upper lip to show the tips of her teeth.

"Nice rack, huh?" Steve commented.

"Why do you refer to women like deer?"

"Not always, sometimes."

"How can I print this out?" Plotnick keenly examined the photo.

"Never mind that. You need to write her back ASAP. She didn't reply to my latest email. I'm afraid you'll lose her!"

"Let me see the last email she sent you."

Steve clicked on the inbox, bringing up the message. The woman had written, "What's with the photo? You want me to get a neck spasm?" The email was signed: "Sonia, from Colombia."

Plotnick was confused. "Whose photo is she reacting to?"

"Yours."

"And why would she get a stiff neck viewing my photo?"

Steve clicked the prompt so the photo filled the screen. Plotnick's image was sideways. "Why? Because her neck probably cramped when she bent her head to make sense of it, being your photo is crooked."

Plotnick stared at Steve. "You, a techie, loaded my photo sideways? What are you a spaz?"

"Actually, some underpaid clerk at CVS loaded it on a floppy for me, which I just inserted into the PC and emailed to her. Besides, it provoked an encouraging reply: 'What, you want to give me a neck spasm?'"

"How is that *encouraging*?" Plotnick shook his head resignedly, pushed Steve aside, and sat at the computer. As long as possible, he silently vowed, he'd keep a sharp eye on what Steve communicated to his dates. He typed a reply. "Sorry about your stiff neck. At least you know where to massage yourself, as a doctor," he wrote. "But too bad you're in Colombia, Sonia. Long distance relationships are, you know, tough."

Nearly immediately, a reply flashed back.

Together they crowded the screen. Plotnick read aloud, "You should try harder to understand my English. I never said I'm *in* Colombia. I live in New Jersey. I *came* from Colombia."

"A mixed message," Steve said. "I detect sarcasm. Maybe not so much the opposite of your ex-wife."

Plotnick typed a reply saying her English was in fact pretty decent for a recent Latin American immigrant. But a week went by without a response. Finally, he zapped her an electronic greeting card from Bluemountain.com. It portrayed a grizzled, emaciated man stranded on a desert island, waiting for a bottled message to float in. He evidently was in the first throes of death.

"Please write back," the card pleaded.

She did. He told her, in turn, of his grudging respect, generally speaking, for doctors. He mentioned his ex-wife hadn't had a real career, or much ambition. He'd made "Judy" the PIN for his ATM card, and came to regret it. For a long time, fresh, crisp twenty-dollar bills smelled to him like breakup, filling him with sadness and longing.

He mentioned how he'd begun writing, putting emotions to paper. He described his minimalist Park Slope apartment, and nearby Prospect Park, featuring the largest contiguous forest in Brooklyn. One could get lost there. From the roof of his apartment building, you could spy harbor ships coming in around the green copper lady, yelping into the vastness. The Gowanus Expressway in the foreground—and beyond, the Verrazano Bridge, touching its reflection, stringing a necklace of pearls to welcome all the immigrants, no matter which political party held sway.

Steve called a few evenings later, managing to get through. "Hey! You on the computer again? All night your phone is busy."

"Can you call me back? I need to send this email."

"No way. I don't trust you. You'll blab. I'm afraid any minute you're going to tell her all your dirty secrets."

"Of course not. I have a much better idea," Plotnick said. "Listen, gotta hang up now. I need to dial up so I can email her this invitation."

"Don't…"

Plotnick clicked on the "Connect" button and ended the call, too preoccupied to care if he sent a screech into Steve's ears.

Several weeks later Plotnick gripped a podium and squinted through his round-rimmed glasses across a dimly lit hall. Once again he checked the photo in his hand against the hip literary types filtering in. He did a quick visual inventory of the coffee bar in the corner, the half-filled rows of folding chairs, the bathrooms off to the left.

"Where is she?" he said, too soft for the mic to pick up.

Plotnick had hoped the casual venue—Eureka Joe's, a coffee house in Chelsea, roughly midway between where he and Sonia Cruz lived—would help cushion the shock. He'd invited his date, without telling her, to a public reading of his tragic life.

He told her they were merely meeting for cappuccino.

A stern-faced, bun-haired woman sitting in the second row, the leader of the writing group Plotnick had joined, which had organized the reading, frowned and gestured to him he'd be starting in a few minutes. Sitting next to her was the reader after him: a wormy man with suspicious eyes who cast wary glances at Plotnick.

Where was she? Instead Plotnick saw his buddy Steve, fresh from work in his Bell Atlantic uniform, stride over from the bar with two beers. "Worst freakin' idea in the world, D," Steve said, reaching up to the stage to hand him a cold one. "I mean, you invited this chick who you know nothing about to listen to you talk about your condition she knows nothing about."

"Would you have me *dis*-invite her?"

Steve stroked his goatee, thinking on it. "No. Too late. But honestly? You're lucky if she doesn't show."

"Why not? I have to be honest with people. I have to be honest with myself." He tapped the sheath of papers in his hand. "I know you're trying to protect me from getting hurt. But I have a good feeling about this one. I see parallels between us."

"Parallels?"

"From the emails we exchanged, our lives are one big metaphor."

"News for you, D. Life is not a poem," Steve said. "It's one thing to ask someone to listen to your literary masterpiece. It's another to get this same person to review your medical records. Unless she's as flexible and powerful as Elastic Woman, you're asking way too much. I mean, disease may come naturally to you, but some of these women want a life-long commitment."

"I sense she's different," Plotnick insisted.

Steve shook his head. "To hell with your instincts. Even tough women break down."

❦   ❦

Even Sonia Cruz. Ninety minutes after setting out in her beat-up Chevy Nova from her sister's apartment in New Jersey, she smelled something burnt and rubbery waft up. An odor disturbingly similar to burnt radiator fluid.

But Sonia chose to ignore this smell and opened the window to wash out the air. Because where she came from you make do with the car you have. You fix your mechanical problems with bubble gum and shoelaces, in a manner of speaking, and a prayer to your special Catholic saint. You struggle to get to where you're going, and Sonia had gotten this far, and she couldn't imagine not going the rest of the way. What was a little burnt radiator smell?

But after Sonia passed the tollbooths and entered the vaguely lit Lincoln Tunnel, about two-thirds the way through, odorous steam eddied through the horizontal slats on the dash. Then: a bang! from under the hood.

The sharp noise struck the chord of a memory.

Bang! Bang!

Sonia stared straight ahead as if hypnotized, fixed on the red taillights of the truck in front of her.

The old scene she'd pictured from police reports flashed through her brain.

Sonia saw not the pair of taillights but … her father's eyes bloodshot with pain.

Slumped against his silver Mazda, his bloodied hands clasped a hole in his chest.

Bang! Bang!

He slumped to the ground. The shooter reached into her father's pocket and snatched his car keys.

Sonia snapped back from the imagined scene and was back in her beat-up car. *Mierda.* She saw the bright red taillights of the truck in front of her—looming large, nearly filling up her windshield.

Dios mio. Mere inches from kissing the truck's rear, she slammed on the brakes—and stopped barely in time.

Cars behind her lurched to a stop too. They honked. And honked. The cacophony grew deafening. But when Sonia tapped on the gas to resume driving and shut up these rude Americans, there was no response. Her Chevy, which usually puttered and complained like a sick motorcycle, was oddly quiet. She pressed on the gas again. *Nada.* Sonia twisted the key to restart the car.

The car had conked out.

She stepped out of the car and opened the hood.

Steam gushed out.

Roughly around the same time, about two miles east on the other side of the tunnel, steam also gushed out—in hissing puffs from the cappuccino cup-shaped clock on the Eureka Joe's wall.

The clock sent a total of eight whispering bursts into the air, indicating the time.

Eight o'clock!

Plotnick tensely shuffled his papers on the podium. As he let more minutes tick past, restless murmurs arose from the audience. Steve came up again, smiling deviantly. Under the bright track lights, his work uniform appeared something like Border Patrol garb. He touched a stubby finger to a brick-sized pack affixed to his utility belt. "Don't worry, Danny boy. If she doesn't show, we'll hunt her down. We'll clip this little device to ... er ... what's her name again?"

"Sonia, you schmuck."

"We'll strap this to Sonia's waist and ... zap!"

"Thanks for the reassurance, jerk," Plotnick said, as his writing group leader glared at him for the umpteenth time, slicing the air as if her hand were a guillotine. "But I guess it's about time you sat in your seat."

The lights dimmed over the audience. Gripping the microphone, Plotnick cleared his throat. It was 8:25 p.m.

"Cancer!" he exclaimed.

Chapter Ten

JUST AS DANIEL PLOTNICK UTTERED THE C word, Sonia entered the half-dark coffee house, hidden in shadows. He evidently didn't see her. But she recognized him and clearly heard the word. She rechecked the photo in her hand against the dark-haired bespectacled head poking up from behind the podium. With his scruffy hair and unshaven face, he looked something like a slacker version of Che, the assassinated Latin revolutionary, whom she greatly admired.

She made her way to a stool at the bar, quietly, not wanting to disturb the audience with her lateness, even if she had a pretty decent excuse. She was lucky she made it at all. *Gracias a dios* she'd had a jug of anti-freeze in her trunk, a towel to delicately unscrew her hot radiator cap, and the steady practiced hands of a primary care physician from Colombia.

"Before my marriage ended in a showdown with police," Plotnick went on, "before I went goth and nearly baptized myself off the GW Bridge—before any of this, there was a single renegade cell. It took root inside me. It grew up fast and didn't stop dividing. It took over my neck. When one day, without warning, there were enough bad cells to form a palpable lump—right by my Adam's apple—and the secret was out.

"This is how it starts sometimes. So innocently. Before you know it, your life has gone into free-fall.

"From there on in, it's safe to say my condition of fast-dividing cells sped up everything else in my life."

He searchingly regarded the audience.

"I was hardly the first: cancer has a history of speeding up seemingly unrelated items. Consider Darryl Strawberry. Already one of the fastest sluggers in baseball history, he led an even faster life after his colon cancer diagnosis: arrested for cocaine possession, soliciting prostitutes, and speeding in his four hundred fifty horsepower Dodge Viper. Likewise for American bicyclist Lance Armstrong, who won more Tour de Frances after an orchidectomy for testicular cancer reduced his carrying load.

"The average American testicle weighs 3.6 ounces."

All around Sonia, murmurs of curiosity arose from the audience.

"But imagine, if you would, it were possible to slow things down. Turn back the clock on that renegade cell. Return it to a pre-cancerous state, in a sense. Imbue it with the power of free will.

"Which, do you suppose, the cell would choose? Life or death? Light or dark? Will it move in the opposite direction from that which it's originally fated? Or go along with the status quo?

"What if, by extension, by some miracle of science, or twist of fate, we could live the opposite of everything we've lived up to that point? What if we had another chance?

"Instead of black, white. Hate, love. Cancer, health. English, Chinese. Just turn off one switch, and switch on another, and voila!

"We all know the theoretical existence of an anti-matter universe existing parallel to our own. Well, here's to the potential existence of the opposite." Plotnick shot his arm in the air. "The opposite! That's what I'm searching for."

He lowered his voice. "Because the opposite would allow me to start over, in a sense, from everything that hurt me."

More murmurs; Plotnick raised his hand for silence.

"And this, my friends, is the prologue to my memoir-in-progress. Tentatively titled, *Never Believe What Your Mother Tells You About Thyroids.*"

"That's not nice!" blurted out an elderly woman in the first row.

"Mom, please," he whispered, but the words audible through the microphone. "It's a *working* title."

Scattered laughter. He addressed the audience, "My story starts innocently enough, a few months after I got married— when my family doctor felt a lump in my throat. Suddenly there I was in the operative waiting room, waiting to get called for surgery…"

His words carried across the room as he described sitting in a hospital gown, ashen-faced wife on one side, divorced parents on the other, waiting for his operation. "I get lumps out all the time, dear," his mother told him, comfortingly. "Just like plucking grapes from the vine." But two weeks after surgery his doctor stared awkwardly across his desk to inform Plotnick, and his wife, he had as much chance of living as dying.

Pobre niño, Sonia thought, picturing the scene. Poor boy.

She gripped her coffee mug tightly, thought of her father, his even grimmer prognosis. Six years earlier, when Sonia worked as a medical intern in a small town in the Colombian countryside, she received word her father was gunned down at his factory in Bogotá. Sonia immediately drove under threatening skies through the mountains and three hours later, as lightning flashed across the sky and the heavens opened up, came to the hospital in Bogotá where she met her distraught family in the waiting room.

She pushed aside a curtain to where her gravely injured father lay, a distant expression in his wan face.

He turned, weakly gripping her hand. It was then he said the last words he would ever breathe.

"You are the responsible one," he said to his daughter.

Plotnick took another sip of water and faced the audience. "And when this prognosis comes, your life goes into free-fall. You find out dark truths you never knew. Your relationships take on a whole new tone."

He told of his wife refusing to accept he was incurable, forcing him into a "liver detoxication" regime. Sonia was reminded of her own involuntary bare-bones diet. Shortly after her father's death, she sat at the kitchen table, pleading into the phone with the utility company. "Give us another week to pay. *Hola? Hola?*"

The front door opened; her mother came in with a small bag of groceries and set them down. Sonia hung up the phone and glanced at the purchases with dismay. "Why all the *plátanos*? Where is the chicken for dinner?"

Her mother choked up—"*No hay dinero!*"—and busied herself by cutting up the banana-like fruit. "Listen," Sonia said. "We'll rent out my room. I'll sleep on the couch. Our family needs to eat more than … *plátanos!*"

"*Soniadita? Escucha.* You do the best you can. I don't want you to feel guilty. Just tell me this: how do you like your *plátanos?*"

Plotnick gripped the microphone. He told of how he rebelled. After all, he had a fifty-fifty chance of living ten years. Not bad compared to, say, pancreatic cancer, which gets you in months. He chose *not* to focus on the little buggers inside his body. He went gothic. The situation exploded when Plotnick came home one night with a silver nose ring—and his allergy-prone wife made him sleep on the love seat in the living room.

Sonia looked off at a corner, remembering how she, too, was forced to spend nights on the couch of her Bogotá home to help make ends meet. One time, around 3 a.m., there was a knock at the front door; a male boarder staggered in reeking of alcohol, with his girlfriend. Passing right by Sonia, ignoring her, the drunk couple stumbled into her former bedroom, shut the door behind them, and assaulted the mattress. Her life was no longer her own.

"Even to this day," Plotnick went on, "I can't believe I changed the locks on my wife…"

Sonia remembered, too, handing over her house keys to her family as she moved out of her house, those tearful *adioses* to her mother and brothers—the dreary moment sitting in an airplane high above Bogotá and gazing out the scratched window, watching the world slip away, the world she'd always known. The mountains around her city growing small and distant as her heart.

A woman in the second row, evidently the event organizer, sliced her hand through the air signaling to the reader he'd exceeded his allotted time, but Plotnick ignored her. He went on to tell the audience of his anger against his father, who pushed him off the GW. "That's why I didn't invite him here tonight."

Sonia's eyes watered with pity for the speaker. After all his pain, to lose touch with his father!

His living, breathing father.

Unable to sit any longer, she stood, moving out of shadows. Her impulse was to sneak out, forgo reliving her grief, the memory of her painful past. But something about Plotnick's next words riveted her:

"My cancer is stable for now, my heart less so. I've learned much from my journey, not everything good, and I'm still learning," he went on. "Even now, I'm haunted by indecision. Where do I go from here? Do I continue to do the opposite of everything so far? Or do I just live my life?"

Plotnick halted in mid-sentence: his gaze locked on Sonia across the room. Murmurs rose from the audience. Sonia could feel his question dangling like an icicle in the air, waiting to be answered. The crowd grew restless, evidently unsure if he had ended his reading on a rhetorical question, one they should answer in their minds.

Someone started clapping, and finally the whole room broke into polite applause.

Plotnick rechecked the photo in his hand, stared back at her. He stepped down from the stage and pushed through the crowd. But someone blocked his path—the same elderly woman, Sonia noticed, who'd scolded him for his book title. His mother. She clutched at his arm; they exchanged what could only be harsh words, faces twisting with tension, but Plotnick pulled away.

Then a short meaty man, oddly in blue-collar work clothes cinched by a utility belt, intercepted him, clasping Plotnick's shoulder. The man's loud comments drifted Sonia's way; she cupped her ear to listen: "Some feedback … from the sound system … lights not right wattage for the stage … odd buzz from the wall there, could be a transformer." He straightened his utility belt, as if emphasizing the point. "Otherwise, your reading didn't suck."

Plotnick shook himself free and resumed his course for Sonia, pushing past audience members.

He stopped not ten feet from her. "Is that you?" he called in a hoarse voice. Their eyes locked again. Her cheeks felt hot: he must have been studying her heart-shaped lips, shimmering with gloss, her olive-toned face framed by a wavy mane with blonde highlights, which she'd spent a half hour styling in front of the mirror. He probably wondered about the book she clasped—with a bird on the cover, entitled *Los Pájaros de América,* the Spanish version of Audubon's *The Birds of America.*

"Is that you?" he asked again, with a tentative smile. "Sonia?"

She was about to emphatically nod but a bun-haired woman walked up to him, blocking Sonia's view of him. The woman was the reading organizer who'd sliced the air with her hand. "Dynamic. Retrospective," Sonia heard her tell Plotnick. "But as I mentioned, long. Sometimes you have to cut out the offending object so the patient has the best possible outcome," she scolded, metaphorically. "You violated the group's NGO directive—Never Go Over. Respect your audience's need for efficiency in story. Don't abuse your privilege, for reading fiction aloud is indeed a privilege in the late 1990s world of multimedia distractions—"

Plotnick left her in mid-sentence, brushing past her, and stopped not three feet from Sonia.

"Are you…?"

Sonia nodded. "The answer is 'both,'" she said, thinking of his question about the path he'd chosen. She pointed to her chest, right above where her heart beat.

Plotnick rechecked the photo in his hand. "Nice to meet you, *Both*. Though I could have sworn from your emails you preferred Sonia."

"Of course, my name is not Both. But the answer to your question is 'both.'"

Plotnick smiled thinly, glancing down at the photo in his hand as if making sure.

"Oh, it's me all right," she said. "How many women with a Spanish accent in this place match the photo in your hand?"

"Well, it seemed you were about to leave. But there is a striking resemblance to the photo. Though the blonde highlights appear new and different. Er, why were you leaving?"

"Because … I can't talk about it … now." Sonia swallowed back the tightness in her throat. "But I have something very important to tell you."

"What?"

"As I say, the answer to your question is both."

"You mean the question I asked at the end of my reading?"

She nodded. "The one you ended with. 'Do I do the opposite of everything I went through? Or do I go live my life?' And I'm telling you the answer is not an 'either/or.' You should do both—the opposite of everything that came before *and* go live your life. Both!"

He led her to the bar, ordered two Coronas, and pushed together two stools. Sitting close to him, she pulled from hers until the cool bitterness calmed her insides.

He wouldn't stop staring at her. "It's good to finally meet you, Sonia. *Me mucho gusto.*"

She laughed. "You complimented my breasts!"

"Ah. Knew I should have stuck with English."

"Just kidding, gringo," she said, smiling apologetically.

"Listen, Sonia. I have to ask you something. How can I do the opposite *and* live my life at the same time? What if living my life is the *same* as everything I did before? You see, this is the real quandary. This is what I can't solve."

"There is no—how do you say?—quandary," she said. "Clearly you didn't live your life before. Now it's time to live the life you should have lived before."

"Oh, boy. But I could have sworn I lived life before. I mean, even with my cancer and my lousy marriage, I still got up in the morning, went to work, argued with my wife, got a laugh from Seinfeld, and got a good night's sleep. I was functional. I took every day and did what normal people do which is basically not much."

"That is not living your life," Sonia pointed out. "That's wasting your life. You wasted your time. You wasted every moment of your wasted days."

There was a hint of indignation in his voice. "How do you know? It's not like you went through it yourself."

"Maybe I have," she said quietly. "Maybe we all do."

He stared at her, and Sonia experienced a rush of longing, as if his gaze were familiar, reaching out to her from another time and place.

Without thinking she pecked him on the cheek. Plotnick seemed a bit dazed, then leaned forward and kissed her cheek too.

"Ahem!"

Sonia spun around: Plotnick's mother stood there, wearing a stern smile.

"Oh don't give me your look, Danny," she said, waving away her son's aghast expression. "So you're not going to introduce me to your date? And after you—my own son—insults me in front of a hundred and eighty people? Naming his book something to make fun of me! And now he's not even going to introduce me? What kind of business is this? Anyway, what are you honey? Puerto Rican? You're so pretty."

"*Encantado de conocerte, señora.*" Sonia smiled politely, extending her hand to shake. "Very nice to meet you. I'm Sonia from Colombia."

"My God. Isn't Colombia on the State Department Watch List?" Mrs. Plotnick clasped her purse with one hand and tentatively reached out to shake Sonia's hand with the other.

Plotnick's gaze bounced between Sonia's face and his mother's, as if trying to navigate the gap between old and new, past and future, perhaps thinking of the growth inside him, the one he wanted to forget, and its relationship to another growth, a more benign one, the one to be nurtured with love and caring.

Chapter Eleven

EVEN AFTER ALL HE'D BEEN THROUGH, PLOTNICK hoped to succeed in love this time. Initial signs were encouraging. He and Judy had talked about everything, including their divorce; Sonia's first language was Spanish, of which Plotnick knew about ten words. Judy was career-challenged, Sonia hard-working. His ex smoked pot; Sonia was a trained medical professional and swore off recreational drugs. The signs started to pile up. Just to make sure he didn't miss any, Plotnick kept a running scorecard in his mind to highlight positive differences, as they emerged, between Sonia Cruz and his ex-wife.

But late one night, after Plotnick returned to his Brooklyn apartment from date no. 6, he grew apprehensive. Foreboding prickled his neck. He made his latest mental notation in a shaky scrawl. For Sonia had told him, over drinks that evening at the opulent Waldorf-Astoria bar, all the soulful details of her dream to make it in the United States.

How she promised her dying father she'd take care of their family but was forced to leave everything she knew in Colombia to immigrate to America to try to pay for this promise. How when the New Jersey night was darkest she found beauty listening, through her window, to the song of mourning doves (a close relative of the pigeon, no less) and sometimes she carried the Audubon bird book, as she had to her first date with Plotnick, as a reminder of this hope.

The situation was too perfect. He felt ashamed to be so focused on his own needs—for being so American. Her perseverance unnerved him. His ex-wife had barely graduated college. By contrast Sonia—a self-directed Colombian who slept on the couch of her sister's apartment in New Jersey and studied medicine in a language foreign to her and cleaned houses to help pay for her medical courses at Kaplan—would probably take care of *him*.

How on earth would he sustain the momentum? The very question sent waves of panic through his brain. He feared moving on too quickly from his failed past could just as quickly lead to crash-and-burn failure in relationship—maybe in his health too.

"Things are going *too* well with Sonia," Plotnick confided in his apartment, a day after date no. 6, to Steve. It didn't matter they'd visited an antique furniture expo in Piscataway on their second date, ate Colombian *ajiaco* (creamy vegetable soup with chicken) in a West New York restaurant on their third—no matter what they did they had a pretty good time. Instead of getting scared off by Plotnick's cancer, she'd taken his hand in hers and mentioned that in Colombia she tended to hundreds of victims of violence. Including her dying father. The tragic personal loss deepened her. She understood life is a gift, as presumably did Plotnick.

"I think it's unsustainable!" Plotnick said miserably. "I don't know how much longer I can keep this up. It's ... like ..."

"You might do the same bad stuff all over again?" Steve said.

Plotnick nodded; Steve rested his goateed chin in his hand, thinking hard on this dilemma. "Well it's good to see you're finally asking the right questions. You may actually *like* this chick. And it's a good sign she hasn't run away from you yet. Listen. Here's my advice. To avoid repeating your past, continue to do the opposite. Just do it more."

Steve suggested ways to do exactly that, and Plotnick felt drawn to the concept like a dying star to a black hole. Bring a yellow rose to the next date instead of the conventional red, Steve suggested. And instead of meeting at a cool café or opulent restaurant in Manhattan, he advised, why not meet in gray, sad Hoboken, New Jersey? It was the setting for Marlon Brando's tough-talking *On The Waterfront* and featured blocks of college dives selling jalapeño poppers, buffalo wings, and the like. It wouldn't be what a chick would expect. "It'll keep her on her Latin toes," Steve added, "slow her down a bit."

And so, for date no. 7, Plotnick brought along a yellow rose instead of the expected red (red, in fact, was the color he'd greeted his first wife with during their early dates). And instead of getting together at a cool café or opulent restaurant in Manhattan, he arranged to meet Sonia in gray, sad Hoboken, New Jersey.

At first he didn't spot her. Ascending that evening from the New Jersey Transit station into a lamp lit plaza, he straightened his glasses across the bridge of his nose and peered down gloomy streets crowded with bars and college kids. He was worried she wouldn't show, perhaps insulted by the low-brow place where he'd chosen to meet.

Plotnick spied an exotic woman with lush hair draped over bare shoulders in front of a restaurant sign. It was her. Their gazes locked as she strode toward him, tight skirt hugging her slender waist, ribbon of lace gift-wrapping her mane of hair. She came up and smiled, revealing her sexy uneven teeth.

They pecked each other on the cheeks in front of a shuttered newsstand.

"Why yellow?" she asked in her Spanish accent, when he handed her the rose.

"Why, you don't like it?" he said, hopefully.

She shook her head and sniffed the petals, dreamily, as if yellow were her favorite color from the time she was *una niña*. "Red roses are so Hallmark, don't you think?" she elaborated in a whisper, lips tickling his ear, as they strolled down the faded promenade and watched out across the Hudson River, reflections of lit-up Manhattan high rises glittering across the inky waters like sequins on a black cocktail dress. "Hoboken's so—how do you Americans say?—awesome!"

Later that night, moreover, when he took her to a Chinese joint in Piscataway, she practically endorsed Plotnick's contrarian approach to relationship.

"Don't slurp!" she told him from across the table as they sipped tea, waiting for their orders. She daintily clasped her own cup, showing him the correct way to hold it. But the very next moment—even as Plotnick touched the cup to his lips in a quieter, more mannered way—she pulled up her shirt.

"Do you like?" she asked, baring her coffee brown breasts.

"What are you crazy?" He set down his tea cup peering left and right.

"You don't like?" Sonia said, frowning with disappointment.

"Who cares if I like? We're in a restaurant. Maybe everyone likes."

"So you do like," she said with satisfaction, slipping her breasts back under her shirt. "Anyway, this place is empty, so don't worry."

"Yeah? Those waiters over there in the booth. They can see. They can see your reflection in the window. Maybe they like. And you call yourself a doctor!"

"So you *do* like?" she persisted.

"Of course I like. What of it?"

Plotnick frankly conceded the point. He thought about it more after dropping her off at her sister's apartment in Jersey and sleeping on it at his own apartment in Brooklyn, and the more he thought about it, the better he felt: the notion of a doctor baring her breasts in a public place right after teaching tea etiquette struck him as oddly appropriate. Her behavior clearly embodied the opposite, not the same, of his non-professional, prudish ex-wife—who happened not to like greasy Chinese food in the least.

Plotnick felt even surer of things after Sonia stayed over at his apartment for the first time. Waking to pale morning light through the bedroom window, filled with sweet memories of their first-ever sexual romp the night before, he sensed change in the air. The clues were everywhere. His bed was empty—of Sonia. Considering their burst of passion eight hours earlier, the room was oddly neat. The lamp that had crashed to the floor, light bulb shattering, was back on the night table, bulb replaced. Their clothes which had practically exploded from their bodies were folded in two neat piles, his and hers, atop the dresser. There was the distant whir of a washing machine, the rattling of a dryer. Everything seemed neat and clean. Something was clearly wrong.

Hearing squeaks through the shut bathroom door, he rose from the bed and opened it.

A half-naked Sonia stood tippy-toed on the sink counter—garbed only in black lace underwear and skimpy bra. Stretching toward the ceiling, she dragged a brick-sized sponge across splotches of mold on the upper walls where shower steam tended to collect.

"Daniel," she said, gazing down at his paralyzed eyes, "when you have a mess like this, you don't want to get your clothes dirty. In my country ... Oh! I'm being rude. *Buenos dias—*" She climbed down from the counter to peck his lips, climbed back up. "—In my country, people who live with a mess have lives that are a mess."

Plotnick stared in awe. *What do I even say to someone who looks like my sexual fantasy of a maid?* After finishing with the bathroom walls, Sonia climbed down and poured several cleaning solutions ending in x—including Ajax, Clorox and Dirt-X—in a blue bucket he didn't even remember owning. She resourcefully mixed them with the toilet bowl brush causing swirls of caustic mist to ominously rise as if from a witch's cauldron.

Afraid of inhaling the stuff, he held his breath and helped a half-naked Sonia lug supplies to the next room. In the kitchen, he exhaled his ocean of air and squatted on a square of tile, contemplating a bead of sweat slipping down Sonia's rippling bare back as she swung a mop back and forth.

"Did your mother clean?" he asked for lack of anything better to say.

She stopped mopping and leaned against the wooden handle. "*Si,* of course. And your wife, didn't she clean?"

He laughed, then explained the most his ex did was infrequently sweep, in female desperation, tumbleweeds of dust so thick she couldn't see her manicured toe nails while walking barefoot down the hallway. "Once in a while, if you call it cleaning."

She pensively spun the mop handle in her hands. "It's true, then, that cleaning habits run in the family."

"I wouldn't exactly consider her family anymore."

"Well your habits must come from somewhere. I hate to think they started with *you*."

After Sonia finished mopping the kitchen, she went through his dresser drawers and closets and threw his old, torn and/or hole-ridden clothes to the floor.

"Er, what the hell are you doing?"

"Cleaning your apartment," she said matter-of-factly, tossing a ragged faded T-shirt onto the growing pile.

"That's my favorite shirt! I finished the 1982 marathon in it!"

She shook her head in disappointment. "Why are Americans so nostalgic? You always feel sad. You still cry for Ronald Reagan. For Argentina. I'm sure your bed sheets have a lot of memories too. How old is this shirt? How old are you Daniel Plotnick? Almost forty?"

"No way. I'm in my upper mid thirties."

Sonia widened a hole in a sock and showed her nose through it like a Halloween mask at a Salvation Army fundraiser.

"And you think it's perfectly okay, to live like this? You must get rid of what's old in your life." She tossed him one of his few remaining sets of clothes. "Put these on, *por favor.* I know a decent mall in New Jersey."

And Sonia grabbed her own clothes, finally covering her half-naked body.

Shortly after noon Plotnick pulled his 1989 Nissan Sentra into the crowded parking lot to the entrance of the Great Paramus Mall. Four hours later they exited the mall back to the parking lot. Birds perched on trees shot up, scattering into sky. Branches of bright leaves snaked over cars. The autumn afternoon was darkening. Plotnick pushed a creaking shopping cart, overflowing with newly bought socks, coats, shirts, and pants, toward his far-away car.

"I can't believe you didn't buy anything!" he shouted above the creaks of the cart's wheels.

"I'm here for you."

"What?"

"I'm here for you."

"That's kind of strange, isn't it?"

"No. I'm here for you."

They finally got to the car.

"So. How do you feel?" she asked, getting in.

"Fine. Like I had an enema. "

"I know what you mean," Sonia said, laughing. "Always I get an enema when I go to Palm Beach."

Plotnick stuck the key in the ignition but didn't turn it. "What?"

"I'm glad you feel fine."

"Oh. Honestly, I'm not sure how I feel. I guess I feel strange spending eighteen hundred bucks all by myself."

Sonia took his hand. "Daniel, look at me! You must not let this dirt take over your life."

"Now only my creditors can. Just like my ex…" His voice trailed off as a memory burned through him. He remembered how he'd forked over $10,000 in a one-time payment to Judy after their separation, the result of a judge's decision that the spouse keeping the apartment should help the other with living expenses.

He shut his eyes against the memory, but only partially succeeded, as a frightening visual metaphor sprung to mind. He pictured a knife-wielding mugger coming at him, pinning him against a dark wall. Holding the blade to his throat. A *female* mugger. He shuddered at the thought. Sure, he'd initiated his divorce. But going through it and cancer at the same time felt like he'd gotten his wallet stolen and, during six hours of neck surgery, his throat slashed.

"You mean your ex-wife didn't shop for you?" Sonia asked, jerking him back to the present.

Plotnick laughed, waving three fingers in the air to demonstrate. "Me and you, we've been going out barely three weeks. In three weeks my first wife-to-be hadn't even *seen* my underwear let alone picked it out for me. To be honest…"

"Yes?"

"…this thing between you and me, whatever it is, gives me the heebie-geebies even though it feels like the opposite of my last relationship."

Sonia took his three outstretched fingers in hers and squeezed hard until pangs of pain shot through his bones. "Ow!"

"Do not worry Daniel Plotnick," she said, in a reassuring tone. "You have so far counted three weeks on your fingers. Before you know it you will run out of fingers to count. Then you will count your toes. When you're done with toes you can stop counting but our relationship may still continue. Then you can relax again."

Chapter Twelve

HE TRIED. HE TRIED TO REASSURE HIMSELF SONIA would continue to be the opposite of his ex, at least judging by how fast the new relationship was taking off compared to his failed one. But in fact, Plotnick didn't relax. Twenty weeks into things, on the same day he used up his last digit—the pinky toe of his left foot—Plotnick received an email from his boss. As he read it, and read it again, pellets of sweat sprang across his forehead and dampened his armpits.

AP was offering him a promotion—to a position in Mexico City as the wire service's Latin American business correspondent. They offered him a nice raise and three months of immersive Spanish classes in Mexico to make him fluent for the job.

Now, there's a certain clause in the U.S. Immigration and Naturalization code which Plotnick vaguely knew of as an editor and reporter for the Associated Press. Sure, a foreigner can try to get permission to study in the United States, as Sonia had, with a student visa. But if the same foreigner leaves the country, coming back isn't easy.

And so Plotnick stared hard at the computer message—straining to squeeze some hidden meaning from it, some mitigating tidbit he might have missed—and sweated some more. Because asking her to keep him company in Mexico meant he'd have to marry her. Or else she'd be forced to say *adios* to her dreams of being a doctor in the United States. Or worse, she'd be forced to say *adios* to him. Either way felt unacceptable.

He went through all manner of arguments to calm himself. *Trust her,* his brain pleaded. He reminded himself Sonia, a doctor in Colombia for eight years before starting over in the U.S., belonged to a profession with one of the highest trust ratios around. By comparison, phone repairmen and bartenders like his buddy Steve probably ranked near the bottom.

Still, Plotnick had trust issues with doctors. Big issues. He recalled how his head-and-neck surgeon had misled him, though unintentionally, about his longevity. *Trust. A tough call.* Of course, Sonia wasn't just *any* doctor, and it clearly was wrong to generalize about an entire profession. But Plotnick couldn't ignore the fact his revised diagnosis by a reputable medical specialist had plunged his first marriage into despair. Now, as he sat at his work desk staring at the computer screen, toying with the idea of starting over in Mexico, cynicism and doubt clouded his thoughts and dreams. He rose shakily from his desk, went to the bathroom, and splashed cold water on his face to try to think straight and stop hyperventilating. After slapping himself on the cheek rather violently, Plotnick decided to cook for Steve: as soon as possible, to illustrate his dilemma through food.

He desperately needed to make a point, and Steve was the right man to direct that point to. He was the sort of guy who showed up, and that's what he'd done, consistently and without complaint, when Plotnick most needed him. This evening was no different. Coming over for dinner promptly at 7 p.m.,

Steve eagerly clasped his pal's hand at the door of the apartment, while Plotnick limply returned the handshake.

"Jeez you look terrible," Steve said.

Plotnick directed him to sit at the kitchen table and brought over a plate of steaming pork chops, sweet potato, and pale boiled carrots. He sat across from his guest.

"Something's definitely out of whack," Steve said, picking up his fork. "You never cook. What's the occasion? Did you invite me over to celebrate you finally did the right thing and called your old man? He's getting pretty serious with my mother. I hear rumblings. She complains you never call your father. You, his only son."

"Spare me the Jewish guilt. Have I spoken to my father recently? Not after what he did to me. Not after what he *didn't* do." Plotnick resignedly shook his head. "Sorry, I have bigger fish to fry. Haven't said a word to him since he literally drove me to the brink."

"Well?"

"Well what?"

"Why the hell did you invite me over?"

"Oh. There's something I need to tell you. That's why I made you dinner."

"You're sending me a message with pork?" Steve sniffed at the rubbery looking chops. "You're telling me you porked your girlfriend?"

"I told you this weeks ago! Not what I'm trying to say here."

"What *are* you trying to say?" Steve knifed a chunk of meat and jammed it in his mouth. "A little dry. And why pork? You're Jewish for Christ's sake."

"I didn't cook; now I do. I didn't eat pork; now I do." Plotnick matter-of-factly set down his own plate of pork and sat across from Steve. "But for all this I don't know how much longer I'll be able to do the opposite of my failed past."

"Opposite?" Steve stabbed his fork and knife at the pork chop, but only with a heavy sawing motion could he cut through it. "What do you mean opposite? Your cooking skills haven't changed one bit."

"Maybe you should try the sweet potato."

Steve placed a forkful in his mouth, then made a little choking sound. "Ketchup!"

"On sweet potato?"

Steve rapidly nodded, not able to speak.

After he brought over ketchup and Steve poured to lubricate the overcooked food, Plotnick blabbed the whole thing. How things with Sonia had reached a painful fork in the road. How his system for doing the reverse in relationship was being put to the ultimate test by a job offer from AP.

Plotnick wanted nothing more than to jet to exotic locales all over Latin America and report back to the rest of the world what was going on there. The job spoke to his craving for adventure, his sense of irony. His desire for literary material. He'd exchange his crowded plain-vanilla Manhattan for a career-boosting, mind-stretching locale. And, finally, he'd remove the pale patina of sickness from his life and replace it with a damn-the-torpedoes robustness, a sense of physical well-being, even super-human strength. For he, Daniel Plotnick, would conquer his personal field of dreams. A field fertile with unrealized possibilities. The opposite of the salted, scorched earth left in the grim wake of his failed first marriage.

But what about Sonia? Who else would keep his wardrobe so spiffy? Certainly not himself. He was entranced by her smile and confidence and medical know-how. Her determination to make it. How she dealt with the death of her father by stepping in to support her family in every way, then striking boldly out on her own. Similar to how he was trying to pick up the pieces of his own life. Besides that, she was sexy.

But to take Sonia with him required Plotnick to take a leap of faith. He'd have to—*No way in hell!*—marry her because her student visa wouldn't let her travel freely across borders with him. Then there was the little issue maybe she'd say No. Just the thought of getting remarried made Plotnick's eyes glisten with fear and his voice tremble with trepidation as he wrapped up his story to Steve.

"Well?" Plotnick said after a moment, when Steve didn't respond.

"What about me?"

"Huh?"

"We've been friends for like ten years. You met Sonia five months ago—over the Internet! Sure, you're building something with her," Steve added. "But you and me, we're *established.* You'd throw us away without thinking twice about it?"

"You're really bothered by that? Hah! You won't even notice I'm gone. I'll be back here for everything medical. I'll be a regular at your bar, just not as regular as now. Best of all, you'll have a place to party. By the time you visit me in Latin America I'll know all the best places. We'll hang out on white sand beaches sipping coconut milk mixed by some exotic dark-skinned babe because that's how Latinas are, they respect their men."

"Sonia's really like that?"

"No. She's different. She respects me, but in a bossy way. Anyway, can you please tell me what to do? You're my Shell Answer Man. I *need* your advice. I'm not giving *that* up."

"Just make sure she's not using you for the Green Card," Steve finally suggested. "Because these Colombians can be a Green Card bear trap."

Plotnick's eyes widened with concern. "A Green Card bear trap?"

Steve squeezed out more ketchup. "It's not the end of the world. But you need to test her to make sure. To see if she'd marry you anyway. Then you can get on with the opposite, as we say."

"You're saying she might be with me for the Green Card? To get her papers? Crap! How would I even go about asking her?"

"Hmm … Have you ever seen a confession scene on Law & Order: Special Victims Unit?" Steve asked, swallowing hard on the last of his pork.

As his friend explained his plan, Plotnick's face lit up. He stood excitedly. He grabbed Steve in a playful headlock. "I'm never going to do the opposite of my every impulse to be friends with you, that's for sure. Because for a phone repairman, you're not too dumb."

"And for a foreign correspondent, you're not too smart."

"*Gracias.*"

"You're not welcome."

Later in the week, Plotnick drove to Sonia's sister's apartment in West Paterson for dinner. She'd invited him over to give him a sense of real Colombian food, and for a second time in less than a week Plotnick blatantly violated the laws of kosher. He ate pork yet again (this time accompanied by fried *plátanos* and rice and beans). Even as he uneasily contemplated what he needed to do, Plotnick had a pretty decent time over dinner trying to explain the basic precepts of Judaism to the four Latin Catholics (the sister, her two gangly teenage kids and Sonia): "It's a sort of Holy Trinity of Gs: God, Gefilte fish, and Guilt."

"Don't forget 'gringo,'" Sonia said, placing more fried pig on his plate.

"Then it wouldn't be a trinity. It would be a quartet or something."

Just then Sonia's sister sang out, "time for *postre!*"—bringing out flan, or custard crusted with burnt sugar, in small glass cups.

Time. Plotnick froze at the word. His head jerked up. There wasn't much time left to get an answer from Sonia. The AP job started in six weeks! He shoveled down his flan and urged Sonia to do the same, insisting they leave to make the movie on time.

Time to get this over with, he thought.

He and Sonia said goodbye to her sister's family; they went down to his car parked on the street. Stepped in. But instead of turning the key in the ignition, he turned on the interior light to harshly illuminate her face.

Plotnick began his interrogation. Thinking on it later, for purposes of his memoir, he realized his technique wasn't quite up to Law and Order: Special Victims Unit. No, the incident was hardly the dramatic highpoint he envisioned. If made for TV, it would have ended up on the cutting room floor. Still, he found himself imagining the scene as a TV script, the bare-bones format helping him to feel emotionally detached so he could cope with the stressful memory.

Here's how it appeared in an early draft of his memoir:

S: "Don't we have to go to Free Willy now?"

D: "Sonia, can I ask you something?"

S: "What happened?"

D: "No big deal. Nothing happened."

S: "Why are you staring at me like that?"

D: "Like what?"

S: "Like you are."

(S and D sitting there silently).

D: "Listen. I need to get something out of the way."

S: "Something happened!"

(D sighing heavily).

D: "Are you with me for the Green Card?"

S: "You think I sleep with you for the Green Card?"

D: "No, what are you kidding?"

S: "What you think? I'm a *puta*?"

D: "No, no. Not at all. Just … this Green Card is a logical thing for me to be curious about. Consider the circumstances. I'm American. You're Colombian."

S: "What?"

D: "I may be terminally ill. You're a beautiful doctor."

(S pondering this for a moment.)

S: "You think I'm a *puta*?"

D: "Are you listening?"

S: "I feel horrible. You think I'm acting? I'm a good actress because I'm faking everything for the paper?"

D: "Please don't think that."

S: "We had such a nice weekend watching the *Terminator 2* movie last time. I can't believe after that you're still thinking like this. I already told you if I wanted I have a friend who can do me a favor, and I don't need to sleep with this person. And believe me, I don't need to sleep with you for the papers."

(S and D sitting silently.)

S: "How low is your self-esteem? You don't think you deserve a nice person because of you? You think you deserve a trashy person?"

(D sitting mute.)

S: "You have same problem as all American men. You only imagine what you want instead of having it. You think all you're good for is a Green Card and money."

(Feebly.)

D: "Not it at all!"

S: "Yes. I know me. You are the same. The same thing with my boyfriend in New Jersey. He was a reporter like you. Take me home please."

D: "Would you marry me?"

S: "Of course not. Take me home."

D: "You are home. We're going to a movie. Would you marry me?"

S: "No. And I *am* home."

(S gets out of the car and slams the door, leaving DP alone).

As Plotnick dejectedly and indignantly drove back to Brooklyn that evening, his first impulse was to give Sonia, and the relationship, acres of space. Don't call for a few days, let her get back to him. If it wasn't meant to be, move on. If it was meant to be, she'd then light on his shoulder like a butterfly. But Plotnick didn't have the luxury of time for this laissez-faire method. He was supposed to be leaving the country, and feared leaving alone.

Plotnick resolved to redouble his contrarian approach. The next day he showed up uninvited at Sonia's sister's door with two dozen yellow flowers and repeated *lo siento* and *yo confío en ti* (I'm sorry! I trust you!) countless times. As Sonia sniffed the roses, losing herself in the soft bright petals, Plotnick plunged into it again, pleadingly.

"We'll go to Mexico for a couple of years. You'll get great medical experience south of the border. My Spanish will be perfect! Our communication will deepen. And you can go anywhere with me. That's the best part. Besides, there's no sound reason I can't fly out of the country. I'm medically stable."

"Daniel Plotnick: you *are* asking me to marry you!"

"Yeah," he said, scarcely believing his own proposal. "I guess I am."

"Why do you say this? You want a Colombian visa this bad?"

Her joking tone was not what he expected to hear. But it evidently was Sonia's way of saying *si!*

"You won't regret it," he said, kissing her tentatively on the lips.

"Don't worry, you'll survive me. I'm not your first wife, so you've had practice," she said, kissing him forcefully back, nearly knocking him over, seeming to read his mind. "I only wish my father were here. To meet the man who dares to marry me. Some people might feel sorry for that man, but not my father."

Chapter Thirteen

FROM A CONTRARIAN VIEWPOINT, THE TIMING was perfect: many months of engagement squeezed into less than six weeks, from proposal to marriage. For that's how soon Plotnick had to pack up and move—these AP postings came and went, as his editor explained to him. Diverging sharply from his first go-round, when it took him nearly a year to decide to get married, and another nine months to plan the wedding and all this meshugas, right down to figuring out where to seat his estranged parents in the dining area, every little detail of the new time frame was compressed.

He made fast work of last-minute routine CT scans of his neck and upper chest and arranged a medical exam as required by his work visa, squeezing appointments with the head-and-neck surgeon and endocrinologist between interviews with the balloon salesmen and the tent company. The wedding was slated for a week-and-a-half before the international movers would whisk their stuff south, in time for the subletters to move in. He'd sell his Nissan Sentra in Park Slope, put a three hundred and fifty dollar deposit on a car in Mexico City and, finally, switch his AP medical insurance from domestic to international.

He made fast work too of the legal requirements. The fourth Thursday in March, he and Sonia visited City Hall in Lower Manhattan where a joyless clerk behind smudged bullet-proof glass declared them man and wife before the law.

"You gave me a big smile in there," Sonia said as they walked out. Clutching the document recording their civil union, she affectionately squeezed her new husband's arm. "You must really love me."

"I feel so happy the marriage bureau seems the antithesis of romantic love. An antithesis to the myth projected by the false catering corporate front that nearly ruined my life. And I love you too."

Sonia gave him a faint-humoring look as if he lived on a different planet but he didn't see it and so they moved on to the next task, submitting those marriage papers to the Immigration and Naturalization Service office at Federal Plaza. Although this getting a Green Card, or permanent residency, could take up to three years, they meanwhile applied for "Advanced Parole" for Sonia—permission for her to cross international borders during her "pending status."

The pace intensified as the day grew closer. Ten days before the ceremony, Plotnick invited Steve over to his soon-to-be-ex-apartment. Plotnick was sweating with excitement when he opened the door. Flushing. Feeling a bit manic.

"You okay?" Steve asked him at the door. "You look—what's the word?—pasty-faced."

Plotnick reached across the threshold, gripped Steve's arm, and pulled him into the room. "I need to know now," he said, gazing hard at his friend. "Are you in with me or not?"

"You coming down with something?"

"No. I'm going all out."

Right then and there, Plotnick let Steve in on his secret plan—not all of it, but most—to make his second wedding the perfect opposite of his first. "Of course I didn't say anything to Sonia yet. Never know how a passionate, purposeful Latina will react off the cuff. But you, Steve, you're rock solid. You I can trust."

Though Steve said he appreciated the compliment he tried to dissuade Plotnick from several of the more extreme notions, but Plotnick was nearly dogmatic in his refusal to backtrack. "Doesn't make me warm and fuzzy but I'll think about it," Steve said. "But I have my own earth-shattering news. First tell me this: did you invite your father and my mother to the wedding?"

"No. Why?"

"Because they just got married themselves. Eloped. My mother called me this morning. They're moving to a condo."

"My God! Where?"

"Pembroke Pines. Florida. They could probably get a good deal on JetBlue for your wedding, so you should tell them pretty soon."

"Please understand, Steve. I'm not ready for this step-brother crap. I'm not ready to talk to my father. It's nothing against your mother. But they're not coming. I'm trying to fight the course of history here. Not repeat the same meshugas trying to seat my divorced mother and father far apart so they don't start fighting or get their feelings hurt. I have too much wrapped up in this current situation to take that one on too."

"It's your wedding, and not inviting them is not what they'd expect," Steve said carefully. "But be forewarned. Your father and my mother will feel it's a slap."

"So what? I've been slapped around more than anyone."

Later, thinking on it, Steve probably should have taken a stronger stand. All those crazy ideas were so clearly a red flag. After all, who knew Plotnick better? He knew his buddy's neuroses in and out, his penchant for extreme solutions to extreme problems. Plotnick had been through a lot, which is exactly why Steve should have been extra-vigilant to try to head things off. Stop his friend's madness before it was too late.

Before Steve knew it, the big day had arrived, and he set out from NYC at dawn on his motorcycle to give Plotnick a hand during those busy hours before the ceremony. As he squinted through Ray-Bans into the bright orange ball bouncing off the eastern horizon, Steve sensed trouble ahead. After ninety minutes on the road he pulled up to the house, a well-preserved Southampton colonial Plotnick had rented for the occasion. As Steve parked on the side, the sonorous morning surrounded him. He walked a stone path past trumpet-shaped flowers and marble statues of angels. It was late spring, air fragrant with pansies and petunias blooming riotously from window sill pots and garden beds. He noticed a few cars in front: select family members had trickled in before the ceremony, several flown in from Colombia, the bride's country of origin, to help set the place up.

Steve went to the oaken front door and banged a heavy brass knocker. He was startled when Plotnick nearly immediately opened up—as if he'd been waiting behind the door for Steve to show.

"It's good to see you, bud," Plotnick said, eyeing Steve's Bell Atlantic uniform, complete with utility belt—in sharp contrast with Plotnick's vanilla tux, white rose pinned to the lapel. "Just like we spoke about. You're a team player if I ever saw one!"

"I'm here for you," Steve said, with a strained smile.

Plotnick gave Steve a tour of the place, chattering on about this and that priceless antique or some other item completely different from his first time tying the knot. After visiting the den, library, and dining room, they circled back to the reception area: the commodious living room, which in a few hours would be bustling with guests. The room was empty of people except for the two buddies—the calm before the storm—but trappings of marital bliss were everywhere: roses and baby's breath in vases, ribbons festooning the walls, a punch bowl in the corner.

"The modern-day decorations mingle somewhat incongruously," said Plotnick, adjusting his tux bow for emphasis, as if he gave old-house tours for a living, "with antique tchotchkes and fixtures. Consider this genuine Tiffany lamp, these sepia-tone photos in frames, the baby grand piano, and fireplace whose mantel holds one of those anniversary clocks … with a pendulum of four metal balls … that never stops…"

Just as Plotnick's spiel was reaching some sort of breathless climax, however, his voice trailed off and he glanced off at a corner, a shadow crossing his face.

"Did you … hear something?" he asked.

Steve listened. "All I hear is old-house creaks and guests chatting through the walls. People taking bets on whether your second marriage will last longer than the first."

"Not funny!"

"Sorry, bud. Just a joke."

"No, what I hear," Plotnick said, "is a kind of... music."

Steve peered left and right. Had the band arrived and started tuning up? But he heard and saw nothing.

"Sounds like the music to a movie," Plotnick went on. "About someone who becomes lost, maybe, while searching for someone even more lost."

"Music to a movie?" Steve whistled. "Dude, you're scaring me. What you're saying is highly specific."

"Scaring me too." Plotnick's arms hugged his chest. "There's like this weird chill down my back. Like my ex-wife is right here in the room with me. Standing in the corner by the punch bowl."

"Punch bowl?" Steve glanced over there. "Listen, feeling edgy is normal for your big day. Honest, I'm glad you're freaking out because it means you're not a total nut-job. Even though hearing music is pretty nutty." Steve lightly slapped his pal's back. "I feel for you, bud. Your ex is like a grease stain you can't get out of your shirt." Steve eyed a smudge on his work uniform and licked his fingers, trying to rub the smudge out. "Though your wedding day would be a good time to finally get her out of your head."

"You know, you're *right*." Plotnick shook his head vigorously. "I'm gonna snap out of it, Steve. You know why? Just being here feels good."

"That's the D I wanna hear!"

"Ahem! Because today's wedding will be the complete opposite of my first. The food. Venue. Ceremony. Of course the bride! Just look at this place. Instead of a schmaltzy Jewish catering hall—distastefully furnished with chandeliers, gold curtains, and mirrored walls—this time I'm getting married in an 1800s landmark house on a half acre in the Waspy enclave of Southampton." He paused for dramatic effect. "I'm gonna succeed in love this time!"

"Well, that's a bit—"

"—and here's my system for success: to move on from my failed past. A failure that started when I married someone who couldn't handle my diagnosis of cancer. So she gets depressed and gains thirty-five pounds—"

"To be fair, she probably lost most of the weight by now. Chicks always do that after the breakup."

"—then she called the cops after I changed the locks on her."

"But *you're* the one who kept the apartment." Steve grabbed his friend's arm and squeezed. "Stop rehashing the past. It's done and over with. Time to mosey on down the road. Hightail it on the next train out of town, as they say."

But Plotnick went on. "That wasn't the worst of it. You know what the worst was? Toward the end, she wanted me to stop being friends with you."

"Christ. You never told me this."

"I didn't tell you because I knew you'd get all upset. Toward the end she felt threatened by our boys' night out on weekends. And Mondays. Occasional Thursdays. But Steve: that's another reason I chose Sonia. She seems to have no problem with you. She *respects* you."

Steve glanced again at his uniform. "Well, I appreciate it. But I think…"

"Anyway, I'm moving on from all that. Together. You and me. And if my theory about opposites proves correct, and I'm confident it will, I could blaze a trail to change the course of

relationships. And stretch the limits of marital possibilities…"
Swept up in in his own dramatic telling, Plotnick added in a
whisper, "…forever!"

"Time to find out how far those limits stretch," Steve said
half aloud—as he watched Sonia enter the room, decked out
in her wedding dress.

Chapter Fourteen

SONIA REGARDED THEM FROM ACROSS THE ROOM. Elegant and sexy in a virginal sort of way, she wore a white sequined dress that hugged her hips, neckline low-cut to reveal olive-toned cleavage. Her dark Latin eyes sparkled as she smiled. Steve liked Sonia, who was a nice package—cute plus professional, with a Colombian accent. Steve felt happy for his friend, even though he felt nervous for him too.

"All dressed up, like I asked," Plotnick whispered excitedly. He'd requested to see Sonia decked out *before* the ceremony, he told Steve, unlike his first go-round, when tradition forbid him from previewing his wife-to-be. "This opposite thing is going great!"

Sonia came over and kissed Plotnick. "*Mi amor.*"

"*Mi amor,*" Plotnick said in a playfully bad accent. "And here's my best man, Stefan, whom you know quite well."

"Of course I know Stefan. How can I not know my husband's best friend? How was your drive here, Stefan?"

"Thanks for asking," Steve said, trying to keep one of his eyelids from twitching. "A little bumpy toward the end, but nothing I couldn't handle."

Sonia moved to hug Steve hello, but at the last moment stepped aside, evidently afraid his clothing might dirty hers. "Did you come straight from work, Stefan? You can change in one of the bedrooms if it's easier," she suggested.

"Er…"

Plotnick touched Sonia's arm. "*Mi amor. Mi cielo.* You know how much thought I've put into this wedding to make it perfect. I sweated every detail!"

"*Si, mi amor.*"

"Well, Steve *is* dressed. This is what he's wearing."

"*Perdón?*"

Steve stepped between them, straightened his utility belt, and gave Sonia an exaggerated salute.

"Steve Kirsch at your service, *señora*! Er, may I point out, as best man at Daniel's first wedding—which bit the big one, I might add—I wore a hundred-dollars-a-day rented tux. But your soon-to-be hubby is moving in the opposite direction, in more ways than one, from his failed marriage. And now … well my work uniform speaks for itself."

"It practically *walks* by itself," Sonia said emphatically.

Steve opened his mouth to reply but was interrupted by the whoosh of the front door opening. Two coffee-skinned dark-haired young men strolled in with smiles and hugs and handshakes all around. Sonia warily ogled their get-ups: jeans, T-shirts, and sneakers.

"Uh, Steve, and Sonia, my cousins Bill and George Cortez from West Paterson. Remember I mentioned their mother's Dominican? They speak Spanish and everything. So they'll fit right in today!"

Sonia eyed them up and down. "Fit right in with who? Stefan?"

Plotnick took Bill and George aside. "Uh guys why don't you help yourselves to a little punch? I'll be with you in a few minutes."

"It's green," Bill observed, gazing at the punch bowl in the corner.

"Exactly," Plotnick said. "Made it myself."

The cousins went over there, tentatively helping themselves to some.

Sonia asked, "What's going on here, Daniel?"

"Calm down Sonia. They're changing into something nice. I wouldn't put you through that. This is why I'm wearing a tux. Even good theories have limits. I've come to realize you have to sacrifice for the greater good."

Sonia took some blush from her purse and hurriedly freshened her cheeks. "I don't understand this opposite thing at all. Changing the environmental conditions won't change our relationship. Your best man looks homeless. Listen, I have a million things to do. Your first marriage must have really messed you up."

"Actually it did. This is the whole point."

Sonia shook her head with disappointment and strode away, trailed by her long flowing gown.

"Well that went over well," Steve said. "You sure she's the opposite of your first wife?"

"Sure I'm sure. I've been over this a million times."

"If you're so sure, why are you testing her?"

"I'm trying to make sure, you know, she's the one," Plotnick said. "And for your information, I didn't tell her beforehand because I needed to make sure."

"Well so far so good," Steve said, sarcastically. "I have to admire you bud. You like living on the edge. This is like watching a new extreme sport take off. You're the trailblazer of remarriage!"

Just then Steve's stomach audibly grumbled. "Speaking of, what's for dinner tonight?"

"Thanks for reminding me," Plotnick said, snapping his fingers. "Time to check up on the food situation."

"What situation?" Steve peeked through the living room into the kitchen. "I didn't see any catering vans outside."

"Steve. Listen closely to what I'm saying. I didn't tell you this before, but … I decided, somewhat at the last minute, we're not doing the cater thing. My second cousin's in the kitchen boiling lobsters right now. Decidedly non-kosher lobsters. Bottom-feeding crustaceans. The opposite of my catered first wedding. I mean, where did kosher get me last time? Last time we had gefilte fish. Nova. Pickled herring."

"Now you're really scaring me. Will you stop this opposite stuff already? What's next, a Buddhist monk conducting the ceremony? Wait. Don't tell me. I don't want to know."

"Er…"

"And not to nitpick, but your food theory is flawed. The opposite of that Jewish fish food is not lobster. The opposite of gefilte fish would be some anti-matter version of a pig. You know—dirty land animal, doesn't chew its cud, no cloven hoof. Kosher vs. non. Molecules vs. anti-molecules. I mean, lobster and whitefish are both *fish.*"

"How am I going to serve anti-matter pig to seventy-five guests? I'm trying to be realistic here!"

"I see your point," Steve said.

"Are you still in with me, Steve? Because you sound like you're wavering. Remember, I can't do it without you. I need your support. I need you to stay strong! Focused! No matter what happens." Plotnick went on in a fake whiny voice, "Please don't leave me all alone!"

Steve stared misty-eyed at his pal. "Just tell me one thing. Will we still be friends when this is all over?"

Plotnick put his arms around Steve's neck in a playful head-lock. "If I told you once I'll tell you a million times. You're not getting rid of me so easily."

"Why not? Wouldn't leaving your longest-lasting friend-ship be the exact opposite of your every instinct?"

"Good point, but—"

Just then Sonia came into the room and walked right up to Plotnick. "Where on earth is the caterer? I keep calling their office but the message says they're not in. They need to set up before the band gets here."

"Here it comes," Steve muttered.

"Uh, there's something—" Plotnick began.

"*Dios mio,*" Sonia said, getting it before he said it.

"Calm down. Everything will be okay. Sure, I cancelled the caterer, but that's exactly why I've arranged to have teams standing by. Everything is meticulously organized…"

Plotnick snapped his fingers with a circular flourish and called over Bill and George, who'd been chatting by the punch bowl.

"Punch tastes interesting," George said, walking up.

"Kind of like broccoli," Bill added.

"Thanks. It's supposed to. Remember what we spoke about over the phone?"

Plotnick took out a sheet of paper from his pocket and unfolded it. "Ahem! The Cheeseballs and Cheese Tray Team. You, Bill and George Cortez, form the core of these all-impor-tant appetizers!" Plotnick glanced up from the instruction sheet and waved it at Sonia. "With complete instructions from top to bottom—all typed up and ready to go."

He handed his cousins the instructions.

"I don't know about this," Bill said. "I never made—"

"Don't worry," Plotnick interrupted, grabbing Bill's arm reassuringly. "As long as you can read English, you'll do *fine*."

"Of course I read English!" Bill said.

"Great! You'll find all the necessary ingredients clearly labeled in the kitchen with the initials CCTT for, er…"

"Cheeseballs and Cheese Tray Team?" Steve helpfully interjected.

"Go to it guys!" Plotnick said.

Bill and George walked away uncertainly toward the kitchen; Sonia held her stomach as if nauseated.

"*Mi amor.* Honey. Listen. For me. My first wedding, which as you know didn't end up well, was catered by some expensive outside caterer. So you see…"

"And now you're taking a cue from *The Idiot's Guide to Catering Your Own Wedding*?"

"In fact, yes! Each carefully chosen team player is responsible for preparation and service of the assigned dish. Long as we're on the subject, how do you say, in Spanish, Salmon-stuffed Zucchini Boat and Dip Team? I'm hoping to tap some of your family to help."

Plotnick unfolded another sheet of paper from his pocket as Sonia stared incredulously at him. Steve took him aside. "Maybe it's time to pull back, bud. You're digging yourself in pretty deep here."

"Okay, okay," Plotnick said, pulling away. "I *understand* your concerns. Sonia. Since your relatives are all Spanish, let's give them culturally specific assignments. Forget this broad brush approach."

He took a pen to the paper and crossed something out and scribbled something in its place. "Give this to your brother and two cousins. From now on they belong to the Cheese-Stuffed Platanos Team. And ask your aunt if she's up for some paella. Just one more thing…"

"There is more?" Sonia said, voice quivering. "Even if I were to accept your *loco* method, there's no time to prepare the food."

"*Loco* means crazy," Steve said, to be helpful.

"There's time," he insisted, "if we all work as a team. This is why I need to ask you a special favor. Would you mind being substitute captain of the Miniature Tropical Fruits Skewers Team? Or the Shrimp and Crabmeat Delights Team? I'll give you your choice. My nephew from Piscataway can't make it. He came down with the flu at the last minute. There should be enough time before…"

"*Loco! Loco!*" she shouted.

Sonia grabbed the food list from Plotnick and reread it to herself, more and more amazed. A glaze came over Plotnick's eyes, Steve noticed—as if his buddy had spied his ex-wife hovering by the punch bowl, perhaps in a ragged wedding dress.

Just then Bill and George returned from the kitchen, not happy.

"Your first marriage," Sonia said shrilly, "must have really hurt you. You are a desperate man. Trying to have your torta and eat it too. I don't know how much more of this I can take."

"Torta means cake," Steve said.

"Si, Daniel Plotnick, it is cake."

"Uh, speaking of cake…"

"*Mierda.* What did you do to our wedding cake?" Sonia yelled.

Bill and George took a step closer. Steve watched Plotnick place a hand on Sonia's flushing cheek, but she brushed it off. "What more could you do to my wedding day!" she said, hysterical edge to her voice.

"Er…" Just then, a girl around seven years old entered the room, pushed past Bill and George Cortez, and tugged at the sleeve of Plotnick's tux. Her curly blonde hair flowed over the collar of her coal-black dress. She carried a basket filled with wilted rose petals, dark as bones, and wore an excited smile.

"I'm all ready, Uncle Danny!" she said with girlish pride.

"Er, hi Suzy," Plotnick said. "Where's your parents?"

"They're getting ready upstairs. But I'm all ready already! Just like you said, I gathered all the dead flower petals I could find and put them in my basket. They're really yucky! I'm going to be the best flower girl ever! I'm gonna throw them all over Aunt Sonia when she comes walking down the aisle!"

"You okay honey?" Plotnick asked Sonia, who appeared sick.

"I need to…" She staggered in her high heels backward out of the room.

"Er, sure honey, whatever…" Sonia ran out of the room as Bill and George drew closer. Suzy nervously backed away and left without her basket.

"What you doing to your wife, man?" Bill said, in a Spanish accent Steve hadn't noticed before. "She don't look too well."

"Maybe this is what she gets for marrying an American," George said quietly, not cracking a smile. "Should have stuck with one of our own."

Just then Sonia came back into the room, dabbing her lips with a napkin. Bill and George walked up to her. "*Soniacita,* we are like brothers and sister. How can we help?"

Sonia started talking to Bill and George in rapid-fire Spanish, too fast for Steve to make out. At one point, tears spilled down her cheeks; Bill and George comforted her with hugs and cast harsh glances at Plotnick and Steve, who stood there awkwardly. Finally, George spoke. "Danny, really! How could you do this to your wife-to-be? Treat her with no respect? Ruin everything important to her on the most important day of her life? Have you no shame?"

"It's … I'm not…" Plotnick's voice weakened. "Maybe I went too far. Maybe I really did it this time. Like last time."

Sonia jabbered loudly in Spanish, with great animation, as the two cousins glared at the gringos.

"What's she saying?" Plotnick whispered to Steve.

"You want the opposite, or the actual?"

"What do you think, wise ass?"

"Not sure, my Spanish is pretty basic, but the idea here is—" Steve edged away from the threesome, who in turn were edging closer. "—is…"

Just then George reached over and grabbed Plotnick's shirt. "It's over Daniel!" Sonia shouted.

"That," Steve said, too late.

George released Plotnick. Sonia stomped out of the room followed by her Latin *compañeros,* who slammed the door behind them.

The room was quiet as Plotnick and Steve wearily lowered themselves to the floor. Steve placed a sympathetic hand on his pal's shoulder. He thought of how it must be for his friend to lose something within reach, something so important, but Steve said nothing, figuring the moment spoke for itself. For a long time the two sat there.

"Maybe there's something to this idea your ex is right here in the room with us," Steve said.

Plotnick nodded. "It's like she's hammering a wedge between me and Sonia. Making me suffer, like I made her suffer when I locked her out of our apartment."

Steve brushed off his Bell Atlantic uniform. "A related question, D: Would your would-be second wife cancelling the wedding as your traitorous half-Latin guests assault you be the opposite? Or the same? Just curious here."

"My would-be second wife tossing me out? And those other things you mentioned? It's unclear. Maybe in the middle? I mean, if you think about it…"

"I'm listening."

"Tossing me out of my second wedding could be the *opposite* of my first marriage because, in my *first* marriage, my then wife-to-be did not in fact throw me out of the wedding. Nine months after the wedding I threw *her* out, in a sense."

"True," Steve said thoughtfully.

"Not that any of it matters now."

"Good point."

"Thanks."

"Don't mention it."

For a long time the buddies gazed off mournfully.

The room door swung open. Sonia stood there clasping a violin in one hand, a bunch of red roses in the other, appearing sexy and pure as ever in her wedding dress.

"Let's go in. The ceremony is starting as scheduled." She slid up her embroidered sleeve to check her dainty silver watch, sniffling. "I wanted to give you up but couldn't. So you are crazy, Daniel Plotnick! I am crazy. Your friend is crazy. My whole family is crazy. Latinos in general are crazy. Besides, anyone who thinks marrying me is the opposite of bad can't be too bad himself."

Plotnick exchanged a glance with Steve.

"The opposite," Plotnick and Steve said at the same time.

"Besides," Sonia continued, "I got in touch with the caterers. Pierre is making an emergency delivery—all in time for dinner. And I picked these roses from the vase in the bedroom to pin on us since you cancelled the florist too."

Plotnick and Steve exchanged another glance. "The same," they said, more softly.

"One thing needs to change. Your best man here, dressed like a homeless person. A suit and black tie for him! My cousin found one in the upstairs closet that should fit Steve well enough. And another thing. My Aunt Anita, who performs in the Bogotá national orchestra, found this violin in the attic. Can you imagine our luck? She knows the Colombian wedding march by heart! She also knows the theme for *Titanic*. So we have lovely violin music to get married to. You see, it doesn't matter anymore you cancelled the band too."

"Oh Sonia!" Plotnick said.

"Daniel!"

"You're ... perfect!"

They hugged tightly. Sonia checked her watch again.

"*Dios mio.* The priest is supposed to get here any minute. Hurry in, both of you. We need to go over the wedding vows with him. He's marrying us in Spanish and English, remember?"

"About the priest..." Plotnick began, in a world-weary sort of way. Just then odd noises, not unlike livestock, came in muffled through the front door. The entrance bell clanged: the door swung open without waiting for someone to open it. Four Buddhist monks in two rows marched in, bald heads meditatively bent, chanting in a dead language. They were followed by an old gypsy woman with a blue glass eye.

She led a donkey by a rope.

Sonia screamed and fled from the room. Steve and Plotnick stared with alarm at the four monks, the gypsy woman and her donkey, who were determinedly marching through the room, circling around, seemingly intent on performing a wedding ceremony.

"I quit," Plotnick said, slumping back to the floor. He shook his head resignedly. "It's over. Totally over. I mean, sometimes you have to embrace your past. Face your fears, not run away from them."

For a long moment neither said anything.

"At least you have something to run away from," Steve said.

"Huh?" Plotnick said, over the clanking of bells on the donkey as it brushed past him.

"You had a wife. You were about to have another. A second chance. I never had any of that. I'd kill for a second chance. But I never even got a first chance."

"Sorry. You never were much of a relationship guy. But it was your choice."

"We all live with our choices," Steve said, as the monks chanted somberly. "And now you have a choice too. To do something about it. To fix what's broke."

"I'm not following you."

"You need to go back in there. Win Sonia back!"

"Are you crazy? And get beat up some more?"

"Now wouldn't that be the opposite of your every instinct? Wouldn't the complete opposite of throwing out your first wife be begging your second wife-to-be to let you stay? The opposite of me, who doesn't even have a choice?"

"Let me get this straight. You're saying, in this one instance, doing the opposite of my impulse would actually cancel out getting the opposite of what I want on an intellectual level?"

Steve nodded rapidly and handed his friend the red roses Sonia had dropped. "Whatever the hell you said. And give her these, D."

He checked out the roses, crunching his face in tortured reflection. "Maybe … you're right. You're saying I should go back in there and get her."

"That's the spirit!" Steve said, encouragingly, getting up from the floor.

Plotnick stood too. He brushed off his tux, straightened his mussed hair, and sniffed the roses. "I'll do that!"

But right as Plotnick stood the monks and gypsy, who'd been circling all this time trying to figure out where the ceremony was supposed to be, barged past the friends, knocking the flowers from Plotnick's hand. Then the donkey walked past, trampling the flowers. One of the monks opened the door deeper into the house, and the entire entourage squeezed through it, exiting the room in the direction of Sonia.

The door swung closed behind them. Plotnick resignedly studied the crushed flowers. Steve ran the tips of his fingers along the violin and bow Sonia had dropped in her hurry to flee.

Steve sighed, staring at the violin. "Did you hear something?"

"Other than braying? Monks chanting?" Plotnick said dejectedly. "Sure. The beat of my ragged heart."

"No. Music. Maybe that music you were talking about." Steve ran his meaty fingers over the heart-shaped violin. It had been years since he'd last touched one. "Used to be second violin in high school," he said half to himself.

"Spare me. I'm not in the mood for your jokes."

"Honest. Used to be really good with strings and chords. Then I focused on splicing cords into telephone jacks, making ring tones. Gotta make a living, right? Now I'm a phone repairman. I quit fiddling around, as we say, so I could fiddle for real."

"You're serious, aren't you? Wow, a whole different side to you. You're an artiste."

"Nah. I wouldn't go that far." Steve unstrapped his utility belt and placed it on the ground. He rested his goatee in the chin cup of the violin and extended the bow. "But I used to be an okay fiddler." After a few awkward squeaks, Steve filled the room with something out of tune, yet melodic. Soulful. He stroked great gasps from the strings. Something stirred in the shadows to the music: he could nearly see it. A person, perhaps. There, behind the punchbowl: Steve could picture the ex-wife slow-dancing—arms waving toward Plotnick like seagrass in a slow current, beckoning him to join her.

Without warning the door swung open, knocking the violin from Steve's hands: the music climactically squeaked to a stop; the image in Steve's mind shattered, replaced by:

Sonia standing there in her gown, looking fabulous as ever.

"The monks speak Spanish," she said.

Plotnick made a little choking sound, straightened a few of the crushed petals on the roses, and offered her the bunch. "I still have Father O'Brien's cell phone number," he said. "Maybe he can co-officiate."

Sonia tossed the roses on the floor, and extravagantly rolled her R's. "Rrrred rrrroses are so Hallmark, don't you think?" she said. "I'll take the dead ones anytime."

Plotnick sighed with relief. "Maybe…"

"That would be…" Steve continued for him.

"Shut up!"

"That would be new. Different."

Plotnick and Sonia hugged tentatively, tightly, then kissed warm and hard and long, as Steve lifted the bow and stroked the violin strings, faster, deeper, until his fingers hurt from the effort, filling the room with gasps of joy and hope.

Something stirred further in the shadows to the music. Out of the corner of his eyes Steve could see the ex-wife take a break from slow-dancing. He saw her turn and gaze sadly at Plotnick, as if then understanding something—that sometimes you need to do the opposite of the expected, do the opposite of the opposite, which is actually the same.

And so she slipped off her high heels and tip-toed out of the room making for the door, flowing away in her shredded wedding dress, forever letting go of the pain that used to be her husband.

Whispering good night.

Chapter Fifteen

THE CEREMONY WENT OFF WITHOUT A HITCH. THE priest gave the vows in English and halting Spanish, monks chanting in the background. The gypsy whispered incantations, Sonia smiling through it all behind her veil, even as the donkey nibbled on her wedding dress. "*L'chaim!*" the Jewish guests said, toasting life, after Plotnick cracked the glass. "*Salud,*" the Colombians added, toasting health. The head monk held up his hand like an umpire. "We wish them *mazel tov,*" he said in a clear, strong, Spanish-accented voice, as Plotnick kissed the bride.

Even the meal went smoothly thanks to the caterer, who delivered the food just in time, serving chicken cordon bleu, wild rice, and choice of snow peas or baby carrots. Dishes were cleared, and right before dessert Plotnick's mother broke free from the seated guests and paddled up to the front, champagne sloshing in her glass. Smiling apologetically, she told her son, "Well *I* made it onto the short list, unlike your father. So put your arm around me, kiddo." Plotnick braced for embarrassment, his back stiffening. She eyed him and Sonia, turned hard under his arm, and twisted to face the guests. Her eyes narrowed, chin changing shape. Silence blasted the room in anticipation.

"A little something I want to say to these two," she began. "May my son's new wife not feed him diet soda. After all that work I did! All those years I fed him good. Better, I don't want to know what she feeds him." Chuckles from the Jews on the left side of the aisle; dumb silence from the right, where the Colombians sat. "My son," her voice loudened, "may he live for a long time. May the pesticides never hurt his liver, which needs to stay strong to fight this pernicious disease of his. May the meat hormones not cause premature sexual development in his progeny. May he take at least one cod liver oil caplet a night. May his red blood cell levels stay high, allowing him enough oxygen to his brain to make good decisions! May he stick around long enough to push me in a wheelchair and pull my plug before I become a babbling idiot! May he overcome his cynicism to life in general. May his wife be a wise shopper but never visit Wal-Mart! Now I'm going to wet my whistle."

Plotnick's mother sipped her champagne. "My son the rebel. He thinks this means I can't tell him 'Shame on you!' anymore. What kind of business is that?"

Appreciative laughter erupted from the Jewish guests on the left side of the room, confused murmurs from the right. Then polite applause all around as mother and son embraced. The crowd relaxed. Sonia translated the mother's speech into Spanish. The Colombians laughed, but more quietly than the Jews. Dessert began on a positive note.

Chapter Sixteen

PLOTNICK SAT NEXT TO SONIA AT A TABLE AT THE front of the room, about to stab his green sorbet with a spoon, when his cell phone rang. Thinking it was his father calling, he debated whether to answer it, but then saw from the caller ID someone else was trying to get in touch.

It was Dr. Douglas. "Oh hi!" Plotnick said. "What? Yeah, just got married, can you believe it? Remarried, actually. What's that? So nice you're calling me with my CT scan results. So personal! Oh. I see. So you're saying what? It's kinda hard to hear…"

Plotnick cupped his ear tighter to the phone straining to hear through the music. "Do you mind speaking a little louder? I'm at a wedding. Whose? Well, mine! One sec, please…"

Plotnick excused himself from Sonia and walked into the adjoining room. The doctor's voice came in clearly now. "Your new scans show significant changes. A background pattern of tiny interstitial pulmonary nodules … representing interval change … since prior examination…"

Plotnick struggled to understand the jargon. "Repeat this please?"

He listened to Dr. Douglas go on for another moment then hung up in a daze.

"Who was it?" Sonia asked when he came back.

"It felt like a wrong number," Plotnick said, getting back to his sorbet, by now a soupy mush.

After the last wedding guest had left or gone upstairs to change or collapsed on a couch or bed somewhere, the two found themselves in the living room, finally alone. Sonia wearily sorted wedding presents as Plotnick anxiously paced.

"Well, at least Mexico has lots of good doctors," he said. "They're like the United States of Latin America. Mexico City is the Upper West Side of Mexico."

"What do you mean?"

"I mean the doctors there can help me make sense of things—while I'm reporting from hotspots throughout Latin America."

"But your doctors are here, in New York. You will see them every six months when we come up to visit our families. What we spoke about."

"Sure. But I'm rethinking things a little since that wrong number I mentioned."

"It was a wrong number?"

"Actually, it was my head-and-neck surgeon. I didn't want to disturb our dessert."

"We are married less than a few hours, and already you're hiding things from me. Why did the doctor call during our wedding? It must be important."

"Something about spots in my lungs showing up on my CT scan."

"Spots?"

Plotnick nodded.

"What did he say about these spots?"

"Each is smaller than a centimeter. They're like a cloud on the bottom of my lungs. A nest of spider eggs. This is how he described it. Lots of little spots," Plotnick said. "I'm not sure what it means."

"Your cancer has spread outside your neck. That's what it means. This changes things! We need to see an oncologist as soon as possible."

"Now how am I possibly going to squeeze that in? I still need to mail a check for the car I'm buying in Mexico City, wire the security deposit for our new apartment there, process the security deposit the subletters sent for our apartment in Brooklyn, fill out paperwork to switch our health insurance from domestic to international. Then I have to update my list of things to do. We leave for Mexico in two weeks!"

"I'm sure you'll have fun," Sonia said, swiping the air with her hand, as if cutting off an essential part of her husband's body.

"You mean, *we'll* have fun," Plotnick said.

"No *you* will have fun in Mexico. Just mail me your used condoms. I will check your levels while you're there."

"Now why would you think to do something like that?"

"If you are having regular sex there, the condom levels will be very low."

"Er, what?"

"I'm not going with you! Not if you don't take care of yourself. First I call back Dr. Douglas to get more details. Then we see the oncologist." She was purposefully thumbing through a phone book. "I know this one on Long Island. Pretty good reputation. So what's it going to be, my new husband?"

"Are you asking me or telling me?"

"Neither. You're the one who needs to make a choice."

Plotnick immediately didn't like the oncologist. Dr. Randolph Muffian said things like, "join my team" and, presumptively, "think of me as your quarterback." After listening to Plotnick's lungs, Dr. Muffian let his stethoscope go slack and had the couple sit across his big desk near a large plaque announcing he headed a statewide group, Solving Cancer through Advanced Research—with the unfortunate acronym, Plotnick noted, of SCAR.

"Doctor," Plotnick said, seeking to take back control of the conversation, "I thought chemo kills only fast-dividing cells. That's why chemo doesn't usually work against what I've got. Medullary thyroid cancer is slow-growing, right?"

"You're asking precisely the right question."

"But what's the right answer?"

The doctor gazed hard at Plotnick. "True, your cancer may be slow-growing. Except when it's not. Is there a risk the chemo won't perform as expected? Yes. But is there a bigger risk not doing anything? This is the question you should be asking."

"What's the answer?"

"Yes."

"Yes what?"

"Yes, yes."

Plotnick leaned back in his chair with a sigh.

"In your case," the doctor continued, "I believe we can have an impact. It seems your tumor has entered a growth spurt. So the chemo could in this instance slow it down. Besides, all medullary cases are different. I had one such patient who had a dramatic response: regression in her lung tumors. You can't ask for more than that!"

Sonia placed a hopeful hand on her husband's arm. "*Gracias a dios.*"

Plotnick asked, "Can you put me in touch with her? I'd like to get a flavor for how big a deal this is, especially with all the side effects."

"Sorry. But she lived a full life. She tolerated the chemo well for two years. I think she worked at the post office."

"She's dead?"

"Yes."

"Of what?"

"Pulmonary aneurism."

"Pulmonary…?"

"Blood clots in the lung. But not a big worry for you, son. Your lung tumors aren't big enough to cause bleeding." He paused, rechecking the lab report on his desk. "As far as we can see."

Plotnick removed his reporter's pad, flipped to a clean page, and unclipped a pen from his shirt pocket. "Maybe there's a way to strike a compromise here. Bear with me on this! First, I want to go to Mexico. Second, you want to poison me. So let's meet in the middle."

The oncologist glanced around his office, as if for help in understanding.

Plotnick explained, "Just give me the recipe, doc. Give me the name of so-and-so chemical compound—Latin names are okay. Just spell them out for me."

"Oh, *that* recipe."

"What other recipe would I be talking about?"

Sonia placed a firm hand on Plotnick's. "Daniel, you must speak politely to the doctor even if you are having a breakdown."

But Plotnick pulled his hand out from hers. "Doctor, give me the names of the drugs you'd recommend. The biggies. When I get to Mexico City—a respected medical hub for Latin America, by the way—I'll visit a specialist to see if your recommendations are a good match."

The oncologist shook his head meaningfully. "It's simply not possible. The chemicals have to be carefully administered, and you, my friend, have to be monitored for side effects. At some point we'll probably need to shuffle the mix. I wouldn't recommend moving to a developing country at a time like this."

"Maybe I don't have time for a time like this."

"If you want to stick around for the next ten years, young man, I suggest you make your disease, not these other items, your priority. Look—" The doctor rubbed his brow with concern. "When I listened to your lungs, they sounded clear. But the spots are tiny and numerous. One day they'll hatch, in a sense. You feel fine today but suddenly you could be battling for breath. My job is to keep you around through that day and beyond."

"Keep me . . . ?" Plotnick checked his watch. "Can't you operate on my lungs? Take out the tumor, get this over with?"

"I'm no surgeon, but you don't want to be ripping these things open. Your spots are small and spread out. It'd be like removing cosmic dust from the Milky Way galaxy."

"Right." Plotnick stood to go as Sonia tried to pull him back to his chair. "What about one lung?" he asked.

Muffian leaned across the desk and locked eyes with Plotnick. "Young man. I know this is a tough decision. Go home, think about it. Talk to other doctors if you want. I'm fine with second opinions!"

As they exited the building to the sidewalk, Plotnick grabbed Sonia's arm.

"We already bought the plane tickets. We leave in seven days. I sold my car. I put a deposit on one in Mexico. The subletters are moving in on Wednesday. They have a legally binding contract. I can't worm out of it. They'll sue! So I'll take the chemo down there. I'll wash it down with tequila. Give me the goddamn recipe—and *viva Mexico!*"

Sonia wrested her arm from him. "What are you talking about? You're not cooking tamales here. These are dangerous chemicals you're putting into your body. There's no way the doctor gives you a recipe."

"Even if he doesn't, what's the difference? I'll get a good doctor down there. And Mexico is famous for alternative treatments."

"The place to get treated is *here*. We don't know anything about the medical care in Mexico. You can't be learning a whole new job and language. You need to focus on getting well."

"Don't you understand? This is my dream. Just like when you came up to the United States to work. You came here to succeed. I'm going there to succeed as a foreign correspondent." Plotnick pointed to his chest, right above where his heart beat. "Following my dream is probably the best thing I can do for my health."

"I didn't risk my life trying to succeed. And I didn't move to the air pollution capital of the world."

"Tell you what. I'll give up smoking," Plotnick said. "This should even things out."

"What?"

"Just kidding. I haven't had a cigarette since my first marriage. I take care of myself."

"You call 'not smoking' taking care of your lungs?"

"Now you sound like my ex-wife."

Sonia placed her fists on her hips. "Yes, you got re-married, Daniel Plotnick. Do you regret it now?"

"Of course not. But let's just say I'm starting to think about *my*self. My cancer threw a monkey wrench into my ex-wife's plans but I never bothered to wonder: What about *mine*?"

They came to the car.

"Open the door," she said.

"I love you. That's why I want you to go with me."

"Open the door."

They stepped into the car. Plotnick started up but kept the car in park.

"And what about you?" he asked. "Where would you be if you hadn't pursued your dream? Treating criminals in Bogotá the police had shot?"

"Even criminals deserved treatment!"

"Yeah, but some were … incurable."

Sonia stared out the window. He leaned his elbows tiredly on the steering wheel. "I'm going, Sonia. I don't care what you say. You need to believe in me—not in some pie-in-the-sky oncologist."

"I do. This is why I care so much."

"Listen. We'll go for a couple of years. You can get great medical experience south of the border. My Spanish will be perfect—our communication will deepen. I'll explore therapies down there. My cancer's slow-growing. I'll be okay till then. Christ, you already got a Green Card—you can go any-where with me."

"And now I'm going home," she said.

He pulled out of the parking space. On the way home, he slowed in front of the Brooklyn Public Library. "Mind if we pop in here a sec?" While Sonia thumbed through Spanish-language *People* magazine in the main reading room, Plotnick labored at the card catalog and bookshelves. He jotted tid-bits of information. When they arrived back at the apartment, he turned on the computer. He sat there for a long time. At one point he caught Sonia peering at him from the bedroom. Then she went back to sleep.

As Sonia slept, Plotnick gazed grimly at the computer screen. Then he turned away and rifled through the stack of library books.

Everything seemed so crazy.

He couldn't stop thinking about his dream of going to Mex-ico. It was in trouble! He felt haunted, too, by Sonia's words. "Yes you got re-married, Daniel Plotnick. Do you regret it now?"

The words echoed mockingly through his head. Just days ago he'd felt so sure of their future together; now he wasn't sure of anything. He fought the urge to say, "Forget it!"—and catch the next flight south of the border.

Still, he tried to focus on the eight ball: find a way to get away from all this confusing nonsense with a clean con-science—and with his wife.

Redoubling his resolve, Plotnick clicked on yet another medical website—right as Sonia called from the next room, "Daniel, you coming to bed? It's nearly midnight."

"Just a sec, hon!" He lowered his voice to a mutter. "More like another hour."

Plotnick rubbed his eyes and rose to make himself a coffee. The hours flew past as he stared bleary-eyed at the screen. By the time dawn pushed back the darkness through the window, he could spell gastroenterologist, endocrinologist, and pulmonary laparoscopy. He'd negotiated the scholarly tiff between head-and-neck surgeons and ear-nose-and-throat specialists. He'd memorized the news headlines on Yahoo, and weighed how death stacked up in the importance of things: bombings and global pandemics competing for headlines with stories on movie ticket sales for *Scream 3*. There was a list, and an order to things, and a scale upon which to judge them—twenty killed in a suicide attack, for instance, ranked at the top. Yet marines had a much higher value—three or four lost in a helicopter crash was a clear news leader. So was "Sierra Leone's amputees find hope in football."

He so wanted to go to Mexico. Three thousand miles from all this craziness. From rules. From the Big Brother of the medical establishment.

Sonia in her pajamas stumbled groggily into the room.

"My God," she said. "Have you even been to sleep?"

Plotnick didn't reply, pressed the Print button, and gave her the printout to read.

"Read 'em and weep," he said.

"What's this?"

"Never mind." He grabbed the printout back and read out loud. "Ahem! This is from Berke's *History of Military Agents Against Cancer*:

" 'The predecessor to modern chemotherapy, mustard gas, was used as a weapon by Germany against French and British soldiers, in World War One, and caused horrific battlefield symptoms such as blistered skin, scalded lungs, and partial blindness. But in later decades, researchers turned these poisons into drugs to harness the despised weapon's ability to disrupt fast-dividing cells. Today, bastard sons of mustard gas attack everything from malignant tumors, on the plus side, to hair follicles to intestinal linings to fingernails on the minus.' "

"The point is … ?" she said.

Plotnick peered up from the pages. "Talk about the industrial-military complex of self-poisoning!"

Sonia sighed. "And how is this related to your decision?"

"Let me ask you a question. Who's to say there's a chance chemo will do anything? Medullary thyroid cancer doesn't always respond to chemo. And who says I'll even survive those chemicals? They're highly toxic."

"How long will you play this game, Daniel? Nothing is easy. The easiest thing is to do nothing."

"And the hardest is taking a risk. Which brings me back to you. How is it you came to the United States? You came without a place to stay, without a job, without health insurance. You left everything you knew. A pretty risky move to pursue a dream, if you ask me. How is this different than me going to Mexico to pursue mine?"

"Stop avoiding the truth of your mortality, Daniel Plotnick. You can tell the character of a man by the path he chooses."

What could Plotnick say to this? Early the next morning he was still sitting in front of the computer when Sonia came in. "And what were you doing up so late last night again?" she said, upset. "You're wearing down your body when you should be making it stronger."

He slapped down a pile of printouts on the kitchen table. "Read 'em and weep, Part Two."

He'd researched alternatives to traditional chemo. Thalidomide, a morning sickness drug—banned in the 1960s for causing deformities in babies—was making a comeback after promising to do the same to tumors. Another experimental therapy, available in Canada, caused fast-dividing cells to implode like cats cooked in microwaves. In another experiment, Johns Hopkins scientists lowered patients' body temperatures on the theory cancer cells froze to death before healthy ones.

"Daniel," she said, "these are all experimental treatments. None have been tried on humans in a scientifically controlled study."

He grabbed the printout and turned to the second page. "Yeah, but one of these studies focused on jalapeño peppers. They have plenty of those in Mexico." The study examined the effectiveness of hot peppers on carcinogenic cells in laboratory rats. The spiced-up rats did best.

She eyed the printout. "Daniel," she said. "You're—how do you Americans say?—freaking out?"

"I'm pointing out *options.*" He strode to the computer and clicked. "Came across another reason I should go. This website, 'Metaphorically Speaking,' gives me an idea. Actually, it adds to an idea I've been cooking up on my own. Actually an expansion of an old idea."

"*Por favor!* Not another idea."

But Plotnick told Sonia his theory of artistic metaphors. Writers need to find a metaphor for their suffering, he said, and express it through art. Only then can they alleviate their pain.

"And what pain are you exactly suffering?" Sonia asked.

"Our relationship, for starters, is suffering."

"*No entiendo*," she said, not understanding.

"It's so simple! I can smell a conflict a mile away. My ex-wife taught me what it smells like. But covering a conflict-ridden country will help fix the conflict within."

"I am not your ex-wife. And our problems are caused by Mexico, not solved by it."

"We're all tense!" he said. "Ever since the oncologist got it in his head to poison me, and I began trying to worm my way out of it, this is all you and me talk about."

"We saw the doctor three days ago."

"Whatever," he said, grabbing the two plane tickets to Mexico from the desk and waving them in her face. "Mexico is a metaphor for solving this situation. I already know my first story when we get settled there. I'll report on how Mexico is like an incurably sick person. The economy is failing, the indigenous poor are getting left behind, the land is drying up, all impoverished by trade agreements that have flooded Mexico with American seed corn. And when my article goes out to newspapers in the United States, the publicity will help raise the hackles of free-thinking people everywhere: triggering an outpouring of sympathy and aid to preserve the native ways that have been around for thousands if not tens of thousands of years."

"If this is the case, you might as well come to Colombia with me. Violence is tearing the place up." Just last week,

Sonia mentioned, guerillas shot up two towns in the south, killing twelve policemen. The government promised retaliation, backed by Black Hawks, which heightened fears of further violence. A former medical practitioner in Bogotá, Sonia understood such concerns more than most. "But all this is besides the point."

She moved closer to him, tapping her forehead to indicate the situation was in his mind. "There's no conflict, Daniel. I am not your ex-wife. You are my soul mate. The conflict is up here, in your head." She rubbed her smooth cheek against his pale prickly one. "We are fine together, don't you think?" She scratched his back, the part below the shoulder blades especially in need.

"Check this out," he blurted out, opening another web page. "'Lonely Planet for Cancer Survivors.' Ahem! 'Cancer cells, like college kids with wanderlust and a Eurail pass, can travel far and wide from their point of origin, latching on elsewhere in a foreign place.'"

Plotnick glanced up. "Don't you see, Sonia? Cancer is *synonymous* with foreign travel."

He waved the plane tickets in front of her again. She kissed him passionately. He pleaded for air.

"I am your metaphor," she said. "You fix your suffering through me. I will be the solution, not the problem."

"Maybe we should go to Belize instead. Or Costa Rica— they're a close second in terms of stability. Or maybe Tibet. It's a very soulful place, right?"

She grabbed the plane tickets out of his hands and ripped them up.

"Just travel *here,*" she said, placing his hand on her chest, right above where her heart beat. "We don't need any lousy plane tickets."

He watched her toss the ticket pieces in the air and pictured the end of everything he'd envisioned. He foresaw how he'd have to reverse what he'd worked so hard and so quickly to accomplish.

The promise and pathos of Mexico itself was fluttering to the floor.

Chapter Seventeen

THE NEXT FEW WEEKS BLURRED BY. PLOTNICK FELT like he was experiencing not reality but a shadowy representation of his life—projected on a movie screen in a darkened theater—in reverse. He informed the subletters they couldn't, after all, have his apartment, bribing them with two thousand dollars so they wouldn't sue him for breach of contract. He switched back his health insurance from international to domestic. He canceled the movers. He forfeited his three hundred fifty dollar deposit on a car in Mexico and scanned the classifieds for a used one in Brooklyn to replace the one he'd sold. He settled back into a position on AP's international desk, editing overseas stories by reporters stationed in exotic places that reminded him, painfully, of the one he'd given up.

His next visit to the oncologist felt particularly surreal. Dr. Muffian set up a chemo schedule, the first treatment set for August 12. He told the couple what they already suspected: all those toxic chemicals could very well damage Plotnick's sex cells, jeopardizing the couple's ability to have children. He urged Plotnick to make deposits in a sperm bank in the four-month window before treatment started, and plan to withdraw the deposits at a later date when he and Sonia were ready to start a family.

A week later, instead of leaving on a jet plane toward his dream job, Plotnick was soaring with Sonia in an elevator to a sperm bank on the 79th floor of the Empire State Building—back then, the second-tallest erection in New York City. Numbers of floors flashed redly past like warning lights.

Plotnick felt depleted. No, he lamented, it wasn't merely the humiliation of going to a sperm bank after his career was sand-bagged. It was the uncertainty of the whole endeavor. His future, including his progeny, was up in the air. In essence, Plotnick would send his "boys" off to frozen exile, as the oncologist advised. He felt bad about this. All his life his sperm had gotten the standard royal treatment. They were born and raised in temperature controlled testicles. Even if he plunged into a cold swimming pool, or entered a shower after the hot water ran out, his testicles would shrink up into his warmer body, fending off the cold.

But no longer. Poor boys! Feet pinned to the fast-rising floor of the elevator, he tried to ease his misgivings by flipping through the sperm bank brochure that Dr. Muffian gave him. The corporate icon was simple enough—a droplet, arguably of semen, encompassing four stick figures, hand-in-hand, representing two parents and their sperm-bank conceived children. But the text was scary. It described how sperm stayed frozen in liquid nitrogen at sub-zero temperatures for many years, if need be.

"One of our unique features is the use of a carousel canister system for deep storage." Much like a merry-go-round, this "system allows the withdrawal of one specimen at a time, minimizing risk of defrosting other specimens." Each stored deposit—they recommended at least seven—ran four hundred seventy-five dollars. Withdrawal cost extra.

The cash outlay merely added to Plotnick's fears. "Are they building a mansion in Antarctica or something?" he asked Sonia, as the bell for the 79th floor finally rang. "Can't we use the kitchen freezer?"

The elevator shuddered to a stop as Sonia pooh-poohed the idea, noting that someone could choose the wrong ice cube for a beverage, especially during the June-through-August party season. Plotnick imagined a roomful of guests commenting that the punch tasted salty.

The elevator door slid open. There was the waiting room. Its windows were narrow vertical windows on opposite walls, with stunning views, one of Manhattan and the other New Jersey. A handful of men sat nervously around. Plotnick filled out forms for twenty minutes. Then a female technician called him up and interviewed him through a round hole in a glass partition.

"When was last ejaculate?" she asked.

Plotnick was confused by the question.

"Last time you ejaculated?" she said louder, seeming to ask the man in line behind him.

"I don't know. Monday?" Plotnick said, reflexively checking his watch.

Sonia threw him a corrective glance.

"Tuesday," he said.

"Tuesday," the technician repeated, writing it down. She handed Plotnick a plastic container. "Don't break seal until ready to use," she advised, reading directly off the label. "Don't want to taint sample. And whatever you do, don't tarry."

Plotnick raised an eyebrow. "Tarry?"

"When you've finished depositing your sample, don't tarry. Just report back to me on the double. The sperm need to be lowered to freezing within ten minutes."

The technician stood, motioning for the awkward couple to follow her down a hallway. She unlocked the first of five doors in a row. "This is where all the magic happens," she said, opening the door. Not much larger than a janitor closet, the dimly lit room barely fit a worn leather recliner, a small table stacked with pornography magazines, and a box of Soft Puff tissues. The technician handed Plotnick a folded white sheet to hygienically cover the chair.

She shut the door, leaving them alone.

Plotnick flipped through the reading material. He came across *Penthouse, Playboy, Barely Legal,* and *All Virgin Revue. Asian Aphrodisiac* brought up the bottom. Making himself comfortable on the plush chair, he checked out an article about Jodie Foster, entitled "Why She Went Both Ways: Confessions of a Bisexual."

"Aren't some of these magazines illegal?" he wondered, but Sonia grabbed the magazine from him.

"Why are you reading this?"

"Er, I'm supposed to?"

"If that's what you think, I'm waiting outside."

"All right, all right. Just let me finish this article I started."

"Do you get why we're here? I mean, you don't even get why we're here!"

"Sonia?" He shut the magazine, put it down, and patted the arm of the chair for Sonia to sit on it, and so she did. "I get what you mean. We're trying to … give it my best shot. The science is amazing but ... unreliable. You see, I get what you're saying. My sperm are ready to take the trip. I'm taking my best shot, literally and figuratively."

"Daniel?"

"Yeah?"

"Shut up."

She purposefully pushed him back into the chair, placed the empty container and two fresh tissues on his lap, and stepped away. "*Ole!*" she said, like a matador taunting a bull. "*Ole!*"

"Oy, I'm gonna do this," he said, self-encouragingly.

Unzipping his pants he reached in and closed his eyes, straining for workable mental images. He could picture diagrams of the female anatomy from his high school health class twenty years earlier. He could hear the heavenly operatic music of Vivaldi float up. *National Geographic* photos of bare-breasted Amazon women spun into view. As the sweetness of Vivaldi soared, Brooke Shields, in skimpy rags straight out of *Blue Lagoon,* shimmied through his mind.

Without warning Vivaldi ripped to a stop, the suggestive images melting away like ice in the Mojave. Plotnick's eyes opened, and he pushed aside the empty container.

Sonia laughed with surprise. "What now?"

"It's that ... I mean, can you really trust these ice cubes? What happens if they melt? Everything's gone. The science couldn't possibly be more imperfect! Our entire future melted away."

"I've been thinking this too. Artificial insemination is no sure thing. The success rates are less than fifty-fifty. But what else can we do?"

"Fifty-fifty." Plotnick felt the pit in his stomach. "Less than my own odds. Where does this leave us?"

Sonia thought for a moment. "There's another option."

"I'm listening."

"Let's do it."

"Do what?"

She smiled at Plotnick like an understanding parent. "Why, have a baby."

"Sonia, isn't this why we're here?"

"No. I mean here. Now."

"What?"

"You know what I'm saying, Daniel Plotnick."

"I do?"

"*Sí.*" She smiled, coquettishly. Consider, she urged, the children who might never eat guanavanas, watch the sea lions in Prospect Park, or eat in Chinatown. Consider children who might never be born let alone have children of their own. "Now do you see, Daniel?"

He sort of did, and grew alarmed. "Sonia. Listen. I'll be on chemo. What kind of shape will I be to run after a kid with a leaky diaper?"

But Plotnick's words rang hollow to a woman who once regularly delivered babies in San Rafael's Hospital in Bogotá. Newborn babies practically leapt with gratitude into her waiting hands, she told him. Once, a pregnant woman from the Colombian countryside who'd traveled two days by foot and horse cart parked herself outside Sonia's hospital and gave birth on the sidewalk, shearing the umbilical cord with her teeth. When Sonia came outside to investigate the commotion, the new mother wiped off her teeth and handed the baby to Sonia to clean up. That's how much the woman wanted a child.

Now the stakes were even higher. "We have no choice," Sonia said.

Plotnick foresaw his own defeat, inhaled deeply, and faced her. They embraced and kissed, falling back into the big chair. They rolled over and over, and you could see them rolling nakedly, and rolling some more, then onto the floor. And the only part of their writhing bodies still visible was their wriggling feet as an unseen camera pulled away, panned across the wall to a drawing on the wall, above the chair, to rest on this charcoal outline of a nude woman, hands on her hips, purposefully gazing off at distant mountains, at the stars. At the promise of life itself.

Chapter Eighteen

THEY TRIED. AND TRIED. BUT DESPITE ALL THEIR efforts—Sonia's meticulous calculations, sexual gymnastics with her husband, and the like—one after another, her Yes! pregnancy test sticks came out No.

She timed her ovulations to his peak sperm counts. Played with positions. On top, bottom, sideways, backward. In bed, on the fire escape under a new moon, two-thirds submerged in lukewarm bathwater enhanced with three-and-a-half tablespoons of extra-virgin olive oil, dash of lemon zest, sprig of cilantro, and twelve basil leaves.

But after two months of earnest trying, halfway into the complex scheme, Sonia struggled against panic. Her brain burned with the knowledge that come August 12, her husband's first chemo treatment, all bets were off. All those toxic chemicals could very well damage his sex cells, as she herself well knew as a doctor. All future progeny blotted out.

And so, minutes after completing their forty-second attempt, sweat dripping down the spine of her back like tears, Sonia roused her husband from his post-coital stupor and pushed him off her.

"There's something wrong, Daniel," she said, fearing yet another negative result. "We've been trying what, fifty-nine days now? How can we get me pregnant when you have this shadow hanging over you?"

He groggily tugged the bed sheet over his nakedness. "What's this about a shadow?"

"I'm saying you need to call your father. That's what's wrong."

"Oh. What does me not talking to him have to do with your not getting pregnant?"

"We tried everything, Daniel. What else could it be?" Sonia leaned over the edge of the bed and gazed at the ceremonial photos she'd arranged on the floor around a brightly flickering candle the diameter of a small water main. The wax cylinder was impressed with delicate white flowers; baby's breath, seemingly the perfect metaphor. But as if confirming her doubts, a sprig flared, sputtered, and disappeared in a puff of smoke.

Unnerved, Sonia went into the bathroom and, after a few moments, poked her head out through the door. "Honestly, you don't have it in you at this point. That's what's happening."

"So it's my fault now?" he called back. "You're the one who made me have my sperm tested. And even though I used to smoke weed on and off, my boys are doing great. This is me you're talking to."

She emerged from the bathroom fully dressed and sat on the edge of the bed. "I'm not talking about your sperm count. I'm talking about context. A child is conceived when the man is ready to be a father. How can you be ready when you don't talk to yours? Do you know how many pregnancy tests I've taken so far?"

"All negative. I know. I'm sure there's a solid medical reason for this. And I want a baby as much as you do. But Sonia. Please understand. Me and him, we've been through a lot. I can't be put through that again."

"You have one opportunity in life to give your father a grandchild. To carry on! Why are you so cynical? You haven't even acknowledged his marriage."

"Cynical?" Plotnick laughed. "You should have seen me back then. I needed his support and he drove me to the Catskills. Talk about cynical."

"I wish my own father was here to help me through my tough times. You are lucky to have yours at least try. And you should stop being as stubborn and old-seeming as you think he is."

Plotnick sat at the edge of the bed, shaking his head. "I'm sorry about your father, but you have to understand where I'm coming from." But she handed him the phone.

"*Llámalo!* Tell him we're coming at the end of August. This way we'll have an announcement to make when we visit. That I'm pregnant. That they're going to be grandparents. It would make our visit really important to all of us. And we can finally exchange wedding presents."

Plotnick chuckled dryly. "Make contact, break the curse, and get pregnant. All in time to make the early bird special at the wachamacallit Chinese joint near their place in Pembroke Pines. That simple. Sure. Whatever you say. Why did I ever marry a Latina! No offense, Sonia."

She handed him the phone again. He pushed it away and instead grabbed her arm and led her to the computer. Plotnick surfed the web and came upon several sites that he insisted supported his point of view, devoted to dubious attempts to conceive. According to PopIcon, an aging overweight former sitcom star was given as much chance of getting pregnant as making a TV comeback. On Wikipedia, he pointed out that King Henry VIII, four hundred years earlier, beheaded a succession of wives who couldn't bear him children, when in fact his own sperm were the defective sex cells.

"I mean, can you prove all these people refrained from calling their father? Has a single historian even speculated about that?" Plotnick added.

"There were no phones during King Henry's time," she pointed out.

"Maybe he used messenger pigeon to reach his dad. Pony Express. Smoke signals."

"Stop making excuses."

"I'm not."

"Then call *now*," Sonia said.

"I'm not ready *now*."

Sonia sighed. She knew when *now* was to the fifth decimal point.

Six weeks earlier, when the oncologist set his first treatment for August 12, Sonia had lost little time lowering herself before the computer keyboard, running her calculations with intense focus, as if about to perform laparoscopic surgery. Everything her medical education had taught her about the infallibility of objective knowledge became part of her toolkit. She forecast her ovulations to the minute, using tried-and-true biological formulas. She calculated, to the nearest quarter-hour, the times and days her ovulations would intersect with his maximum sperm counts, the equation complicated by the fact he was making sperm bank deposits every few days per the oncologist's advice.

She even enlightened her husband about the mechanics, hoping to get him more intellectually involved. She made sure Daniel was squeamishly familiar with how a woman's ovulations were signaled each month by an increase in her blood's progesterone and estrogen levels, spurring one of her several hundred remaining eggs to break through the membrane of the ovarium encasing the egg. The egg would start a twenty-four-hour journey into one of her two fallopian tubes (diagrams of which, he told her with a disdainful smirk, resembled a smiling deer with antlers), prodded along by cilia waving like tree branches in a typhoon.

But now their journey to conception seemed, to Sonia, to have hit a roadblock. Even though her husband agreed to go through with it, he now sounded a defiant note. Despite her repeated pleadings, and pleas from Steve over beers and over the phone, Plotnick refused to call his father, making this or that excuse. And with every negative reading of each pregnancy stick she tested, Sonia's sense of resignation deepened. His refusal reminded her of life's fragility instead of its resilience. While she knew intellectually chemo stood a chance of curbing the malignant growth in her husband, she felt in her bones that more than chemistry was required to seed a benign one in her.

Finally, Sonia had had enough. Thick into their sixty-eighth attempt, right when Plotnick was blurting out "yeah, that's right babe, just like…" Sonia stopped rotating her hips, dismounted, reached over, and placed the phone on the clammy chest of her gasping, red-faced husband.

"*Llámalo,*" she said, meaning business this time.

"Hey! That's dirty pool."

"Enough wasting our time. Wasting our future because you are a stubborn mule," she sternly went on, brushing her mussed hair from her eyes.

"Look at me!" he said, gesturing at his lower body. "I can't make a phone call in this condition."

"*Ya no más!*" Enough!

"You're crazy…" But Plotnick's words trailed off. Evidently determined to cling onto a last shred of dignity, he rotated his fisted hands in a circle as if mixing a cake. "If I call, do you promise to go back to doing that thing you were doing?"

"What thing?"

"You know, the cake mixer thing with your hips. As soon as I finish my phone call?"

She smiled kindly at her husband, who wanted to minimize his losses. He wiped the sweat out of his resigned eyes, zipped his pants, and punched in the phone number.

"Thank God I got his answering machine," he whispered to the ceiling. "Uh, hey Dad? This is Danny. I know it's been a while, but … well I wanted to …"

"Say it!" Sonia said.

"We're thinking to visit and want to know when's a good time. And say hello to Mona!" Plotnick spit out the words in rapid succession, then hung up.

"Got his machine," he explained, glancing away as if trying to purge his memory of the phone call.

"Why didn't you tell him we want to see him at the end of August? After finishing what we need to finish?"

"Are you crazy? I need to prepare to go see my father! I need therapy, a Xanax prescription. I can't go on a moment's notice." He sighed as if all the bad stuff in his life, from infancy on, began and ended with his father.

Sonia bent her ear forward, signaling to her husband to follow her every word. "*Escucha.* Listen. August is less than two months from now. We no longer have time for self-pity. The time is *now.* Anything less is making excuses."

"Can't we discuss this later?" he asked. "After, you know … ?"

Like a good Latin wife (but also thinking it might make him less resistant to her entreaties), she restarted attempt no. 68, gyrating her hips like a two-speed cake mixer. When things on the bed were well underway again, however, the phone rang. The message machine clicked on.

"Hey kids, good to get your phone call! I was in the john. Mona and I were wondering when the hell we'd hear from you. It's been what, a year? Two? Didn't you kids get married or something?" his father added, in a sarcastic tone.

The call ended; Sonia again dismounted her husband. "Phone him back right now," she ordered.

"Don't leave me hanging again!"

"We already spoke about this. We are trying to make a child, not just sex."

Plotnick struggled to re-zip his bulging pants. "I'll call him back from the next room. In case I say something I might later regret, I can't have you lecturing me. Just talking to him is tough enough."

"You are strange, Daniel Plotnick. A man should be happy to talk to his father. You know how happy I'd be to talk to mine?" She handed him the phone and he walked off shame-faced, punched in the phone number, stepped into the hall-way clothes closet, and shut the door.

Plotnick remained there for several minutes. His voice was too muffled to hear through the closet door but Sonia could picture her husband staring into the blackness of the closet chewing on his fingernails. Listening distantly to his father say niceties back.

Five minutes later he emerged, pale and shaken. "The only time they have free is the beginning of August," he said woodenly, as if the trauma of revisiting his past had severed his voice of emotion.

Sonia touched his arm. "It's nice you finally talked to him, Daniel. But the beginning of August is so soon. That weekend I reach my peak of peaks. I thought you were going to make it so we could first finish things up here?"

"Well, it's a done deal. They're going to Club Med the rest of August. Hah! Like they really need a vacation from their permanent vacation."

"Well, it'll be tough, *mi amor*. The window of opportunity is smaller, but hopefully the shadow is lifted. Anyway, let's get back to work."

"Sorry, I lost the mood," Plotnick said.

"Who cares if you're in the mood? This has nothing to do with your mood. This is serious business," she said with annoyance, throwing him down to the bed.

"I … can't right now," he said. "Calling my father is like the complete opposite of an orgasm. Why don't you kill some time and buy the plane tickets. Until I get the feeling back? I did my part by calling him. What's fair is fair."

Sonia wearily stood, went to the computer, and clicked her way to a travel website. "Did your part?" she said, researching flights. "Hah! You haven't even started your part. Now we have thirty days instead of forty-five to make a baby." She jotted down a phone number of a travel agency, made a phone call, and hung up. "The plane leaves on August second. So the first thing we need to do is invest in a new mattress."

"Are you kidding? We're already doing it like bunnies."

"Better than doing it like a seal, like the way you always did it, about twice a year, before we started trying. But now the real work starts."

True to her words, Sonia redoubled her efforts to make a baby within an even narrower window of time.

After buying the plane tickets, she grabbed her purse and drove to Sleepy's and bought a fourteen hundred dollar mattress that featured, in her medical view, the correct cushioning and springs. She made additions to the ceremonial perch on the bedroom floor, setting against the candle several photos scissored from *Pregnancy Monthly,* and a thumbnail-sized illustration of her special Catholic saint. Sonia figured she needed the extra help. She was thirty-five years old, getting on, at least by modern child-bearing standards. Emotionally speaking, moreover, her husband wasn't exactly supportive. Cheerful about their future he clearly wasn't.

Seeking to enlist his support, she urged him to read an article in *Pregnancy Monthly* about the influence of moon cycles and Kenny G songs. She gave him a coupon for twenty percent off Vitamin B12, shown to bolster semen motility in rhesus monkeys. She reminded him he didn't like condoms anyway. He'd long complained they felt too tight and rubbery on him. Except for the lambskin ones, which never really protected you anyway. You could drive a truck through those tiny holes, he said.

How many times had she pulled out her calculator? She lost count.

One evening, prior to attempt no. 87, Sonia gazed through misty eyes at her husband sitting next to her on the bedroom floor. "I don't have a way to give my father a grandchild. But you do. Get on your knees. Because I love you, Daniel, and so I will ask for you."

"Ask what for me?"

"*Mira.*" The illustration of her Catholic saint beckoned from where she'd set it, wavering in the lit candle's gyrating shadow. She made Plotnick kneel before it and she did the same, firelight dancing across her supplicant face and his bewildered one. "*Podrias ayudarme a darle un nieto al padre de mi esposo?*" Can you help me give Daniel's father a grandson?

Her elbow sharply jabbed his ribs. "Add something to the blessing!"

"Uh. Please?"

Sonia translated on his behalf. "*Por favor, Padre.*"

A moment later, she climbed back to the bed, pulling Plotnick up with her. "We already waited long enough to see what my saint's answer is." She impatiently spread her naturally tan legs across the new mattress she'd bought to speed things along. As moonlight streamed through the bedroom window, Kenny G playing gently in the background, candle flame doing the flamenco, Plotnick obediently crept in next to her bare body, which coiled like a question mark to the question she'd sought her saint to answer. The meekness of her husband's approach during no. 87 made her feel comparatively strong and full of conviction, as if she might be able to conceive a child with a little push from her saint instead of a big one from her husband. But even though her climax was extra-profound, which Sonia interpreted as a positive sign, the bed's frenetic motion ominously snuffed out the candle, a potentially negative one.

After sex, Sonia gazed over the bedside toward the floor and saw the dark smoke streaming up from the candle wick as if from a funeral pyre. The omen suggested that perhaps prayer wasn't enough. Or Daniel was too much of a mouse to her dominatrix, her outer environment not in sync with his inner. Or the other way around? Anyway, she recalled reading something to this effect from a Buddhist philosopher she'd studied at her Bogotá university who claimed the act of human conception transcends time and space, the start of new life connected somehow to the very conception of the universe.

As her post-coital husband softly snored from the bed, Sonia relit the candle and rested beside it. By the flickering light, she opened a book she had picked up from a stoop sale a few days ago: *The Big Bang Revisited,* by Oliver Heinz. She leafed through and came to a chapter on "Geography's Surprising Role."

Maybe it's true, she thought. *Madre Naturale,* Mother Nature, could help restore balance in their sexual relationship, harmonizing it with the metaphysical environment they now journeyed through.

So one coolish summer evening, she led her husband up a three block hill, from their apartment on Sixth Avenue to the border of Prospect Park, and together they surmounted the perimeter's old stone wall. They entered the main meadow. A bright moon fermented and bubbled in puddles of shimmering white. Somewhere here, she figured, was a geographic center. A fold in the Earth's energy field. A place to productively make love.

"There's like, no privacy here," Plotnick said, as car-honking, kids' shouts, and an ambulance's distant wail floated in and out, leaf shadows trembling across moonlit patches of lawn like frayed remnants of modesty. "What's this theory of yours again?"

Brushing past him, Sonia pointed her flashlight toward a stand of sycamore trees, then at a page in the book. "Over here, the underground is like a magnet," she said eagerly, peering up from the text and accompanying maps. It was 9 p.m. According to her calculations, her eggs were ready to jump off the proverbial high diving board.

She purposefully grabbed Plotnick and pulled him down to the ground. He assumed his usual subservient position, on bottom, but she thought better of it, wanting to personally feel closer to the earth, and switched positions so he, for a change, was on top and she on bottom. Blades of weeds pressed into her bare buttocks, pebbles pinching her spine. Settling into the overused park lawn, she grew familiar with the lay of the land. She peeled off her Victoria's Secret bra and revealed to him her perfumed moonlit breasts. Then he was in—rocking her back and forth. She sucked in air and gripped her husband's ears, tensing her inner thighs. As his thrusts drove her deeper into the ground, her legs forced him to recoil so he moved with her, their breaths quickening together in a climactic tremor of flesh against flesh.

Afterwards, the situation was reminiscent, at least to Sonia, of the collision of Tectonic plates in South America hundreds of millions of years ago, delivering a mountain range in what is now Colombia. Their ninety-first attempt was consummated.

"Padre, how much longer," she said afterwards back at the apartment, softly, reverently kneeling before the candle flame, "until Harold Plotnick gets a grandchild?"

She taped a list of supportive English words to the computer, in case the Higher Authority was bilingual, consulting frequently on spellings with her dog-eared Spanish-English dictionary. Whenever she sent an email or studied online for the medical boards, these words helped her keep a keen eye on the eight ball. Some words she added to it, some she crossed out.

They included impeccable, unparalleled, singular, remarkable. Fascinating, doubtless, fastidious. Studious.

Sonia later added, "Sexy." "Titillating." "Stitches wounds." She wrote this last attribute, which reflected her hope that her child would study to be a doctor like her, in pink marker using giant swirling letters.

She used these and other flattering words to describe their future child who, sadly and despite all their best efforts, didn't yet exist.

After another two weeks went by with nothing cooking in the proverbial oven, Sonia suggested Plotnick was holding something back. "It's time to tell your father how you feel. To *connect*. You can't have a relationship if you're a block of wood."

Plotnick shook his head. "I'm not about to have a heart-to-heart with him. Just dialing his number is tough enough."

"I'm not talking about a heart-to-heart over the phone." She checked her calculator. "The time has come for you to be honest right to his face."

"You mean…?"

"Yes," she said. "It's almost time to have sex in his house."

"So soon?"

"It's out of our hands now," she said in a far-away voice, a part of her having already landed in Florida.

Chapter Nineteen

WITH FOUR DAYS TO GO BEFORE THEIR FLIGHT, Sonia tapped her Casio to calculate, again and again, the ideal time and date for sex. She scattered the ivories like Liberace giving his finale performance at Carnegie Hall. There was a spring in her fingers as she worked the keys. Soon the results were set in stone. Only Sonia knew. It was her game to play.

Though at first resigned and reluctant to copulate at her in-laws, Sonia did some last-minute research and learned hot sticky weather could very well boost her fertility. Dubbed "Land of Perfumed Air Conditioners" (LOPAC) by the AARP, southern Florida summers were rivaled in the U.S. only by those in Texas, Louisiana, and Arizona, according to the Internet.

She read and reread her $9.95 pocket guide to *Secrets to Sperm-Travel Success* by Bernie Plotnick (no relation to her own husband). Written during the American author's trip to Kenya, where he met his wife, Cassandra, Bernie and the thirty-five-year-old woman conceived biracial triplets in three weeks flat. High outdoor temperatures, according to the author, supported child-bearing elsewhere as well. Parents in hot places had tons of children: an average 6.2 per family in Malawi; 5.4 Ivory Coast; 4.7 Uganda. Conversely, Canada's was 2.2; Iceland's 1.7; and Russia's 1.2 (extrapolating, frigidity was evidently heightened by cold, and Sonia didn't disagree).

Leaving fifty-five degree weather one early morning from JFK Airport, the Plotnicks caught a flight to Florida and landed in eighty-nine degree weather.

"*Estoy lista!*" I am ready. Sonia said this from the rental car's passenger seat, as Plotnick drove them from the airport to his father's condo in Pembroke Pines, her *Sperm-Travel Success* pages rippling in the hot hurricane pouring through the car's open windows. She grasped for comfort her Accu-Rate indoor thermometer (though mainly suitable for turkey basting) she'd brought for the upcoming days and nights she anticipated of literally heated love-making.

"My eggs are dropping, and the weather's great!" she yelled, feeling more positive than she had in weeks, raising her voice against the wind whooshing through the Marge and Bernie's rental car—the basic model, thanks to Sonia's meticulous planning, lacked air conditioning—as they passed repeating cookie-cutter retirement communities on the way from the airport. "But I thought Americans would try to live better," she continued. "It's so flat here! Bogotá has mountains covered with pine trees all around it. Every Sunday the mayor closes the roads and people with bicycles come out. I would like to show that to you one day, *mi amor*. It's like a big party for all the people. The mayor of my city is so popular for this reason."

As they drove through the high-security Las Palmas entrance under the blazing midday sun, keeping to the five mph speed limit, the waterspout at the center of the complex's artificial pond caught her eye. Water spurted feebly upward every twenty seconds or so—a metaphor, she figured, for the ejaculations of old people in their last sexual gasps. Each of these eight hundred sixty-four palm-shaded apartment units featured balconies with ready views of this fountain, a symbolic reminder of an old man's lethargic penile pulse. Sonia turned pensive. *This is what we must do. Be strong. Before we grow old and the world grows old. Be strong. Before we wake up and it's too late to bear children.*

Gazing at her husband through the sweat rappelling past her eyes, Sonia thought of her own father. When he was killed at age forty-eight, Eduardo Cruz was barely a decade older than her own husband now. He was a macho Colombian guy. He sported a dark narrow moustache in deference to his movie idol Charles Bronson. He refused to back down that night his car was jacked, according to the police report.

"Come get them," he purportedly told the criminals, reflexively tucking the keys deep in his pocket.

The only reply was a single index finger pressing and re-pressing the metal trigger. Even now, Sonia could imagine hearing the ricochet of bullets, one of which went crazily in his chest. Pow! Pow! Her eyes moistened. Because a man cannot be grabbed back. Because the most solid thing she had of her father was laser-etched in the blood diamond of male ego. Just a memory now. Staring blankly at the feeble fountain, she felt alone in America. Not yet working. Helpless to even pay off her father's debts that piled on when his factory went bankrupt after he died. And now ... now she was two thousand miles from his gravestone, married to a man who might not help her bear children, a man who himself might not make it—who, finally, fell out of touch with his own father, just as Sonia had.

"Do you love him?" she asked her husband. They stood in front of the door of his father's condo, gazing at Home Sweet Home embroidered on a small pink heart-shaped pillow hanging from the door knocker. Plotnick's hand, about to press the buzzer, stopped in mid-journey.

"Who?" he asked.

"Your father."

"Oh. Love's a tough word."

"What do you mean?"

"Well, of course he's *okay*. He divorced my mother, which probably smoothed the way for my own divorce. So he can't be all bad."

"All fathers are difficult. But do you love him?" Sonia smiled encouragingly. "This is the most important."

"The real question is this," he said. "Am I ready for an old Jewish guy who whines non-stop? That's the question you should be asking."

"You didn't answer me."

"I suppose I do. Love him, I mean. When he's not a maniac pushing me off bridges."

Sonia clasped Plotnick's elbow so they faced the door together, as a couple.

"It's a start. Just remember. No matter what, he's your *father*."

He rang the doorbell.

The condo door swung open. A rush of mechanically cooled air prickled Sonia's thin South American skin. Standing there, resolving in the interior gloom, was not Harold but his wife Mona, with sympathetic eyes and frosted, freshly coiffed hair. "Well hello newlyweds!" she began cheerfully, but was cut off by a male voice roaring somewhere behind her, "What the hell kind of emergency number is this if no one ever answers!"

With an apologetic smile, she welcomed them inside. Hesitating for a moment, they stepped through the doorway, where they could hear and vaguely see Harold yelling into a phone from the next room, veins popping out of his neck.

"Honey, the kids are here!" Mona called.

Harold slammed down the phone. "Great. I was just finishing up."

He came up to them in the foyer, face twisting between a smile and a scowl. He chewed on something. "My dentist is getting rich off me but can't answer a goddamn emergency phone number on Saturday. My temporary crown fell out and I have no idea what to do with the glue the dentist office left me, but…"

"Ahem!" Plotnick said.

Harold's expression softened. "Anyway, who wants to hear an old man's meshugas? How are you, Danny? It's been too long. And here's your better half! Didn't you guys get married or something?"

As Mona and Sonia watched, Harold made a motion as if to embrace his son, but Plotnick instead put out his hand. Harold extended his too. They shook and stepped back again. There was a brief awkward silence, the group standing there in the foyer, getting the feel of things. Sonia spent this pinch of time reminding herself why she'd come—to get pregnant!—with the help of two estranged blood relatives who couldn't even hug. Her father-in-law's features resolved in the foyer. Harold Plotnick appeared like he'd once been taller than his son. His shoulders stuck in a forward lean. His hair still plentiful but an odd bronze tint, face brown and deeply lined as if he'd fallen asleep under tanning lamps. The transplanted New Yorker in Florida was a common breed to Americans, perhaps, but largely unfamiliar to Sonia, like an alien from a planet that lost its protective layer of ozone.

The moment ended as suddenly as it had begun. "So nice to see you too." Sonia said smiling at Harold and Mona, willing away the icy feeling inside her and tenaciously transcending her feelings of alienation. She warmly kissed each of their cheeks, French-style, hewing to her country's tradition of respecting in-laws nearly as much as your actual parents.

"Here's your wedding present," Sonia said, handing a box to Mona. "Finally you can enjoy it!"

Harold read the box. "A year's worth of smoked lox," he said, furrowing his eyebrows with concern. "Won't it go bad? I mean, how much can a person eat in one sitting?"

"It's not the actual lox. It's a gift certificate to Ben's Kosher deli." Plotnick sighed. "There's a Ben's right here in Pembroke Pines."

"Thank God," Harold said.

"Hey, Harry," Mona said, squeezing Sonia's hand in thanks. "I like this one. She's practically Jewish."

"A keeper for sure. Hey! Anyone for a glass of milk? Cookies? After such a long trip…"

"I made chopped liver sandwiches," Mona protested.

"Right. You kids are right in time for lunch. We've been cooking lunch for you two years now."

"One year," Mona corrected.

"Two, three, what's the difference? So what, he didn't invite us to the wedding? The important thing is we're all *here*."

Harold handed a wad of cash to his son. "A hundred bucks. It would have been great to be there to give it to you personally."

"You're giving us a roll of cash?" Plotnick said.

"Cash is a legitimate wedding gift," Harold said.

"*Muchisimas gracias,*" Sonia said, giving her husband a look.

"Anyway, why you two still standing in the doorway? Come inside. Cool off! Something to drink?" Harold said.

Tightly hugging herself, Sonia stepped inside. "Maybe hot chocolate? It's a bit cold in here."

Chapter Twenty

THAT AFTERNOON AND EVENING, AS HAROLD COMplained about his broken crown, Sonia silently fretted about the impact of the air conditioning in the apartment, and in the Chinese restaurant (the four of them having caught the 4:30 p.m. early bird special), on the mood of her eggs and her husband's sperm. Deepening her concerns, she discovered the Accu-Rate thermometer she'd brought was not in fact accurate, registering an out-of-whack ninety-two degrees in the frigid Chinese restaurant. Evidently, the device was turkey-specific. Fortunately, the evening was very warm.

After dinner, the four of them strolled around the artificial pond with the spurting fountain, taking in the twilight. As Harold went on about his conditions, which in addition to his sore mouth, included arthritis in six fingers (up from four a few years earlier) and lower back flare-ups, his stock fell in Sonia's mind. Staring gloomily off, she could picture this chronic complainer losing patience with his own grandchild. Yelling at his *nieto* playing in the dirt. Covering the kitchen chairs with towels to keep from getting baby food on the furniture.

After all, he is American, Sonia reminded herself, gazing down at the concrete path passing underfoot as they began a second orbit around the pond, Harold's voice buzzing in the forest of her thoughts. *Americans don't like to touch. They don't let themselves be touched. Because they might get dirty. Must make everything sterile, like a surgeon's knife. This is how Americans are.*

"But enough about me. Something I have to show you," Harold said. Everyone stood still in the path. There was the ghostly far-off splashing of the fountain. Harold slowly raised his hands in the air, letting them drift like clouds against the darkening sky. Alternately bending one leg and straightening the other, he swiveled his hips in slow motion.

"What the hell?" Plotnick said. But Sonia put an index finger to her lips, shushing him. Harold was practicing tai chi. She remembered the stress she suffered from working at hospitals back in Colombia. She'd learned the concept of "chi," a vital energy running through the body to improve the energy circulation throughout to every stiff, dark corner. How this energy helped save her from overwhelming tension. Again and again. Maybe now too.

She felt her mood lift in tandem with Harold's gestures. Following his lead, she poked the air with her hands, tracing the dim stars appearing in the sky. She languidly wriggled her hips as if doing the salsa underwater.

Harold smiled. "Tai chi got you too?" He fluidly relaxed his arms, coming in for a landing. He slowed his swiveling. So did Sonia, feeling less anxious now. Harold explained, "For my pain and stress. Keeps the arthritis at bay. Along with some other things. So your old man doesn't complain so much."

"He'll be seventy-two in February," Mona said.

"Shhh!" Harold said.

"They say if you do tai chi one hundred days in a row, you gain back eight years of youth," Sonia said.

"Of course," Harold said. "That's why I got into it. Soon I'll be sixty-four again. Danny used to complain I complain too much. Well, now I'm doing something about it." He pulled a spray can out of his pocket.

"Thick 'Ems?" Plotnick said, leaning close to read the can. "Something you bought from a TV infomercial?"

"How did you know?"

"An educated guess. You seem to exist at the juxtaposition of Eastern wisdom and commercialism."

"Whatever you mean, I'm sure it's not a compliment," Harold said. "Anyway, once a week I spray my hair. They call this color 'Bronze Blast.' But I prefer to call it 'Iced Cappuccino.'"

"Mohave Mist is what I call it," Mona said, taking Sonia's arm in a sisterly way. Harold Plotnick blushed in the moonlight. He mentioned to the young couple his toenails were "nearly perfect now," recovering from a recent flare-up of the mottled purple condition that had arguably contributed to the demise of his first marriage.

"Check them out," Harold said, reaching down to take off his shoes. "This anti-fungal medicine I'm taking works like a charm."

"This isn't a barn, Dad."

"Have it your way! But listen to this. Despite everything, I sometimes bleed in the shower."

"When he's peeing," Mona added.

"This is the point of what I've been mentioning. Trying to care of myself." Harold grabbed Sonia's arm. "As a doctor, do you know about this bladder problem?"

"Of course. I can show you on the Internet."

"You know this from the computer?"

"No Dad, they don't have computers in Colombia."

"Don't embarrass me in front of your wife," Harold said. "I can still wash your mouth out with soap. It's enough you shut me out for three years!"

"Eighteen months," Mona said quietly.

Still they fight, Sonia thought. *Nearly two years have come and gone, but still…*

Father and son glared at each other through the gloom, but Sonia stepped between them. "You haven't seen each other for so long. This is how you talk? And my own husband! All you have is bitterness in your voice, Daniel. If there's something you need to get off your chest, say it."

"Hear, hear," Mona said, supportively.

Plotnick took Sonia aside, speaking too softly for his father and Mona to hear. "This isn't Truth or Consequences. I can't blab out the first thing that comes to mind."

"Then blab the second thing," Sonia whispered back.

"I could sure use some coffee while we're figuring out where my damn pee blood is coming from," Harold said. "Let's go inside."

Sonia spoke again into her husband's ear. "We'll pick up on this later. But start practicing now. We don't have much time."

Back inside, while Mona put up a pot, Harold started up his Web TV, a sort of large-type version of the Internet, popular back then with the far-sighted set, as the four of them sprawled out on the kitty-cornered beige couch to watch. Sonia couldn't help but link the couch color to bland American culture. *Is this what I'm bringing my child into? No risks. Nothing out of place.* There were those prints of classic American scenes symmetrically displayed on the wall above the couch. *Yet I know our child will know the world. He will not decorate with nothingness. I will make sure of it.*

As if willing her wish to open up the world, the World Wide Web shimmered across the twenty-six-inch Panasonic. Sonia rested the wireless keyboard on her lap and Googled "blood" and "urine," clicking her way to a "Bladder Logic" website.

As Mona poured coffee, Harold asked, "Dear, would you make yourself useful and get my glasses?"

"I *am* being useful," Mona said, dropping a lump of sugar into his cup.

"I know, dear. You're actually very useful. They're on the dresser!"

A minute later she returned with his glasses. "Isn't she a great wife?" he smiled, putting them on. "Okay. This the website? Says when people exercise too much, people like me, especially old people like me, the two sides of the bladder can rub against each other, and the lining bleeds." He let the glasses slip down his nose and turned to Sonia. "Am I reading this correctly?"

Sonia nodded. "Do you exercise in addition to tai chi?"

"Shuffleboard doesn't count," Daniel commented.

Harold's ears turned pink. "For your information, I've been walking."

"Briskly!" Mona added brightly.

"Briskly," Harold agreed.

"Dear, maybe you should stop briskly walking for a few days," Mona said.

Sonia clicked on a small bladder-shaped icon, making it spurt red.

"See a urologist as soon as possible," advised the "Helpful Tips and Hints" tab in bright orange letters.

Harold harrumphed. "No way I'm seeing a urologist. Last one I saw nearly sent me to the hospital."

Plotnick screwed up his face. "I see specialists all the time. I'm seeing my oncologist next Friday. What's wrong with a specialist? The state of Florida is crawling with specialists. I mean, isn't that one reason you two moved here? No offense."

"Anyone take cream?" Mona asked.

"What are you so scared about? Do you know how many doctors I've seen for my cancer? I get pricked and poked once a month. A week from now I'll be poisoning myself, losing my hair, and throwing up. How can you complain so much?"

"Daniel! Start being nice right now," Sonia said.

"Wait. He's right." Harold sighed. "I'm sorry you're going through this, Danny. I've … been meaning to ask you about it. It's just we've been out of touch for so long. Exactly what does a urologist involve, Sonia?"

"The test is standard. He would insert a five-inch sterile metal probe into the penile orifice to take samples checking for infection and inflammation. Then he puts another probe…"

"Enough!" Harold raised his hand. "How about some Turkey Hill vanilla ice cream?"

Mona was already getting the bowls.

As Harold scooped out some real vanilla bean, he said, "I appreciate your advice, Sonia. I'm going to tone down the exercise. Do you like to walk or jog? If you want to use my exercise shoes these next few days, they're good to go. My feet are small, like Danny's. Probably fit you. The same as size nine, woman's."

"Um, let me see." Plotnick read the side of the package containing his father's anti-fungal medicine. "I don't want my wife walking around with…"

"I'm not contagious, for your information."

"You said that in the Catskills—and now the fungus is back!"

Sonia scrunched her eyebrows in concern. "Both of you—you worry about nothing. I mean, I'm not going to get fungus. And Mr. Plotnick, I want to be honest with you. You are fine without hair dye." Sonia sat Harold and her husband on two executive chairs on either side of her. "There are more important things you two should be talking about."

She bent her husband's ear. "Tell him about us."

"Do we really want to get them involved?"

"Never mind. I can see you are *un pollo*. There's no time for indecision."

Raising her voice to a commanding tone, Sonia addressed Mona and Harold. "We're going to have a baby."

"Trying, would be the operative word," her husband said.

"This is *wonderful* news," Mona said.

"I don't know what to say!" Harold said.

Mona gently grasped Sonia's hand. "How far along are you, dear?"

Plotnick exhaled tensely, as if sifting the air through a sieve. "No. You don't understand. You think you do, but you don't. And the worst part is, my wife seems determined to make you understand."

"You are right," Sonia said. "If it's going to happen, they must know everything. There are no more secrets. The journey is out of our hands now."

"This *journey* has been out of my hands since the day we started on it."

Harold and Mona's eyes had been flitting back and forth between Plotnick and Sonia, as if watching a Ping Pong game.

"What the hell are you two talking about?" Harold asked.

"Don't be shy, *mi amor*," Sonia said.

"No way I'm telling them. He's my father!"

"Exactly my point. That's why it's time to be honest." Facing Harold and Mona, Sonia placed a hand on each of their shoulders. "The thing is…" she began.

"We haven't made a baby yet," Plotnick blurted out.

Sonia smiled. "And we need to make one here."

"Oh!" Mona said in surprise.

"Here, as in where?" Harold said.

"*Tu hermosa casa.*" Sonia reflexively spoke in Spanish, as she tended to do when anxious.

"Your house," Plotnick translated.

"Your pretty house," Sonia corrected, politely. She touched her hand to her husband's flushed cheek. "Didn't this feel good to say?"

Plotnick groaned and collapsed back on the couch.

"I see," said Harold. "So you need to have sex in my house?"

"And why is this?" Mona asked, gazing at Sonia with friendly curiosity.

"Danny starts chemo August 12. I ovulate tonight."

Plotnick sat up attentively on the couch. "This is a bit soon, Sonia, don't you think? I mean, we just got here."

"Sorry, *mi amor.* I've run the calculations more times than I can count. It's beyond my control."

"Well, if there's anything we can do let us know!" Mona said, helpfully.

"Of course there is," Harold said. "I'm already cooking up some ideas."

"No." His son slowly rose from the couch and stood. "No," he said, louder. "This is not happening. I will wake up from this nightmare any minute now."

"Snap out of it," Sonia said. "This is for real."

"Just one rule," Harold said. "Keep it down. The wall's paper-thin. The condo board can be strict about these things."

"Like there's really a lot of noisy sex in this place," Plotnick shouted.

Sonia held her husband's arm, smoothing the minute hairs on his hand. "*Mi amor. Mi vida. Cálmate.*"

"Calm down? How can I calm down? My father has this habit of barging into my life, when it's convenient for him. And what happened last time? He drove me to the brink. Literally!"

Silence filled the room, save for the distant gurgling of the coffee maker in the kitchen.

Harold said, "So I'm the crazy loon? You call that little stunt you pulled locking your wife out the apartment normal? Couldn't you have a normal divorce like mine?"

"Yeah, and you didn't even show up to mine," Plotnick muttered. He turned to Sonia. "Thanks so much for bringing us together. I mean, this is fantastic."

"This won't do at all," Sonia sort of agreed. "Let's try again."

"I'm not even sure why Danny's pissed at me," Harold said. "Two years later and all I hear is battery acid in his voice. I mean, what did I do, murder him?"

"*Almost.*" His son clenched his fists. "You sure had your priorities, didn't you? Dating! Then you took me to the Catskills because *you* wanted to get lucky. And I'm the victim of it all."

Sonia said, "But your father was trying to help you, give you what he thought you needed: a helping hand. To make up for the time he wasn't there for you. And you hate him for this? That's the only strange part here."

"And where was he when the police showed up? He never shows up. It's that simple."

Everyone stared at Plotnick, as if saying: It's not so simple.

"More coffee, anyone?" Mona asked.

Sonia touched her husband's arm. "Daniel, how can you expect to take care of our child, as a father, when you won't let your own father back into your life?"

"*Oy vey,*" Harold said, clutching his head.

"Please, Mr. Plotnick," Sonia said. "Danny doesn't mean…"

"It's not him. It's my damn crown. Crap!" He held his jaw. "And my dentist won't answer the phone. Who do I even ask?"

"Let me take a peek. Say ahhhh."

He did. Sonia peered in. "Hmm. I need … flashlight and something to dry the glue. Would you let me take care of this, Harold? It's a simple procedure."

"Glue? Flashlight?" Harold said. "Still, I don't know where else to turn."

Sonia barked orders. "Mona! Bring a flashlight and blow drier. And the temporary glue the dentist gave you. And some cold water in a glass. Daniel, get over here."

"Cold water?" Mona asked.

"I'm thirsty from all that coffee," Sonia explained. "I have a hard time doing minor procedures on a mouth when mine is dry."

Mona disappeared and came back with the equipment. "Good," Sonia said, sipping from the glass. "Now, Daniel. Come here and hold this like a good son."

"Er, hold what?"

She grabbed his hand and led it to his father's mouth. "Hold this open as I operate."

Plotnick drew back in shock. "I'm not touching that!"

"Daniel! Your own father! You should be ashamed of yourself."

"No way. I can't." He was mumbling now. "I mean, this is gross. We don't do this in the United States. Please understand, Sonia. You're a highly educated woman."

Mona came over. "I don't mind substituting. I'm used to Harry's mouth."

"*Gracias*, but I need you to hold the blow dryer. A woman is better at aiming these things. Daniel. *Vamos*! This is something only you can do."

He sheepishly strode closer. Sonia grabbed his reluctant hand and thrust it close to the side of his father's mouth. She ringed his index finger and thumb, showing him which moist fleshy part to clasp.

"I don't know why…" His voice trailed off. Plotnick stuck his fingers in his father's mouth and clasped the cheek. He pulled the cheek to one side as Sonia instructed him. He clamped his eyes shut as if avoiding the midday sun's glare. "You almost finished?"

Sonia laughed. "I just started!"

"Argh…" Harold added.

Chapter Twenty-One

THE PROCEDURE LASTED FORTY-FIVE MINUTES. First, her fingers worked the existing crown side to side until it loosed. With a final tug, she removed it. Mona dried the surface with the blow dryer; Sonia layered the glue on top and then gingerly positioned the temporary filling, firmly pressing it down.

Mona blasted the blow dryer anew to dry the whole thing.

Finally done, Sonia handed Harold a mirror. "This should hold until the dentist can see you," she said.

"I'm letting go now," Plotnick rasped weakly.

Sonia nodded. As Plotnick unclamped his fingers, collapsing into a chair with exhaustion, Harold blurted out through stretched lips, "Danny, thank you for marrying that woman."

"I used to be an emergency room doctor in Bogotá," she explained, blushing with pride. "Daniel, doesn't that feel good? Finally, to be connected with your father."

"*Literally.*"

"Where you going?"

"Nowhere. Just to the kitchen. To scrub my hands with Brillo."

When Plotnick came back from the kitchen, Harold said, "How can I thank you both?"

Sonia said, "But you see, *we're* the ones who need to give thanks. To both of you." She explained her theory of needing to reconcile with the previous generation in order to connect with the next. "So before I ovulate, Danny and Harold had to…"

"And they did!" Mona exclaimed.

"Danny and his dad are better now. Better with each other. Aren't you?"

Her husband exchanged a glance with his father, half-heartedly nodding; Harold stood from his chair, grabbed hold of Mona's hand, and solemnly cleared his throat. "Danny! Sonia! We're ready to help in any way possible. It's already decided. We'll help you *try*."

"With everything we've got," Mona added.

A horrified look came over Plotnick's face. "No," he said, soft-voiced and ineffectually.

"One hand washes the other," Harold said.

"Yeah. That's why I used Brillo."

"Let's get started," Sonia said, briskly ignoring him. "There's no time to waste!"

They were as good if not better than their word. That evening, Harold lent them one of his favorite albums—a debut collection from Peter Sinatra, nephew of the late crooner—with yellow marker highlighting the cover song, "Soil of Destiny." He inserted the CD in the music player in the guest room, all ready to play. He climbed a small stepladder and reached into the back shelf of the linen closet and pulled out some dusty black light bulbs. He screwed them into the guest room lamps, set to illuminate the room in suggestive purplish hues.

Mona, evidently inspired by her younger days in the 1960s, ran out to the twenty-four-hour Wal-Mart and bought a lava lamp that she placed strategically on the night table. Giving it a test run, she pointed out how "pregnant" globs of oil floated lazily up and down the glass cylinder like possibly pregnant tropical fish. She also managed to find (at Wal-Mart, no less) incense sticks drenched in pheromones, natural agents the human body produces to attract the opposite sex. She placed a lighter shaped like a lipstick compact next to the incense stick holder, ready to get things going at precisely the right time, with precisely the right type of flame.

At 8:43 p.m., everything set, Harold and Mona stood at the door, wishing the kids luck. Harold said, "I already switched off the AC. Too bad they don't have heating units in Florida."

"Yeah, too bad," Plotnick said.

"Yes, this *would* be nice," Sonia said.

"Well, I guess we'll be—" Mona said.

"Wait," Sonia interrupted. "Do you have a thermometer? Mine's broken."

"Just what I use for monitoring meat on the outdoor grill," Mona said.

"Let's give it a try. Hurry. There's not much time."

Mona went and brought back the meat thermometer; Sonia placed it on the sill of the open window.

"My fingers are crossed for you," Harold said.

"Both of our fingers," Mona said.

They shut the door. Sonia opened the window wide and placed Mona's thermometer on the sill to measure how quickly the hot night sucked the cooler air from the room. She switched on the lava lamp, lighting globs of oil with tropical colors, shifting from blue to violet to red to yellow. Sweating heavily, her husband unbuttoned his shirt. When without warning, the door opened again, Mona's head popping in.

"Here's some matches for the incense," she said. "Oops! I see I already left a lighter."

"Good luck, kids!" Harold said from the background, pulling Mona from the doorway, getting in a last minute peek himself.

Just as they closed the door again, however, Harold pushed it back open, snapping his fingers. "Thought of something else." He stepped into the room. "Two words. Tai chi." He strode up and clasped Sonia's shoulder. "Remember: the energy from within!"

"My God," Plotnick said. "Are you going to give us an actual demonstration?"

"You—both of you—need to open up the inner energy channels. Unleash your power and exchange it. With each other."

"Yes, Luke Skywalker," his son said. "May the force be with us."

"And that's all we have to say," Harold said, making for the door.

"We can only hope."

"*Gracias*," Sonia said. "I mean it."

"*De nada*, Sonia. Despite whatever Danny says." Harold finally left.

The younger Plotnick shut the door and locked it, saying, "Wow, never suspected the old fart knew Spanish." Sonia returned to her preparations and lit the incense, filling the room with honey-sweet smoke. She switched on the black lights, brushing the room in evocative hues.

"Your teeth are purple," Plotnick said, smiling falsely to show his own. "Very attractive from a sexual standpoint."

Sonia checked the clock radio on the night-table. She joined her husband on the bed, stripped and ordered him to do the same. He touched her bare skin gleaming in the black light, and wrapped his arms around her waist.

Sonia rechecked the time. "Save your feelings, husband; it isn't time yet. We have a few minutes to spare."

"Maybe we should play some Parcheesi," he joked.

"Maybe…" Sonia's gaze turned inward; she gently pushed him off. "No. I have a better idea. I will ask you something instead."

"Anything, wife."

"Do they have good antique shows in Florida?"

"What kind of question is that? This place has the largest concentration of old people in the world."

"We should help your father and Mona shop for some furniture, don't you think?"

"I think they're pretty set from a furniture point of view. I mean, once an old person buys a couch, that's it. My mother still keeps the plastic slip cover on the one she bought with my father right after they were married."

"Now isn't that something?" Sonia's eyes moistened. "I mean, can't you imagine a bone china washing bowl, on top of an embroidered ottoman in your father's living room? A couple of hand-made chairs instead of that horrible couch?"

"But why…?" He handed her a tissue to wipe her tears.

"I keep thinking: my own father would never shop at Seaman's. Seaman's is so *American*. Is this the world we want for our child?"

"You say it like it's a bad word, Sonia. One day soon you'll be an American citizen."

"My father…"

Sonia gazed out the open window at the darkened pond, its fountain splashing anemically in the moonlight. "I mean, here we are," she continued quietly. "In America. To fix what broke over there. My father would want…"

Plotnick placed his hand on hers. "Sonia. My father is not your father. He comes from a totally different planet. But this doesn't mean the world he lives in is any less legitimate."

She gazed at him for a long moment. "You are so right. For a change. You learned something today. I think you are starting to understand."

"Anyway, I'm sorry about—"

"Don't be sorry anymore. Just give me a child!"

He drew back from her.

"I'm sorry I spoke like that, Daniel. But I am so serious. *Escucha*. We must time our noises so they are blocked by the splashing sound of the lake fountain," she said, hurriedly tapping the tiny keyboard of the calculator, "so your father and step-mother won't get in trouble with the condo board. We can start at 8:56. Assuming it gets to eighty-nine by then. Oh! We're missing music."

The thermometer read eighty-five. Face glistening red with heat, Plotnick pressed play on the CD player. Peter Sinatra softly bellowed: *The sway of the trees, the look in your eye—how the cumulus clouds roll across the sky…*

Sweat beaded Plotnick's upper lip as steamy air belched through the wide-open window. "It's like an oven in here," he said, the hair on his head standing nearly straight in the heat and humidity.

"My eggs are nearly warm," she said. "Time to get going."

"I'm boiling!" he agreed.

... tell me you're ready to take the leap
that your love for me is more than skin deep:
I'm like a condition you don't want to treat
A cancer you hesitate to beat...

The clock clicked to 8:56. Without warning, she pulled Plotnick to her left breast (not coincidentally one of the body's two largest sweat glands) and pressed his face into it. After a minute or two he returned to Sonia's eye level, gasping and squinting as if temporarily blinded.

"Would you do that thing you did...?" he began, hopefully.

... so take my hand and start to swim
the ocean that beckons from within...

Sonia began the cake mixer thing, even as she kept one eye fixed on the thermometer, the other on the clock. She did that thing he wanted so well it probably wouldn't have seemed, to a casual observer, like a cake mixer anymore.

... together we'll go, you and me
to sow the soil with our seed...

As the thermometer's red bar sped north of ninety degrees, Sonia wriggled her hips even faster. Her husband's face lit up like the sun. She felt blue crackling sparks discharge from his fingernails into the skin of her back.

"Tai chi!" Sonia gasped.

... to sow the soil of destiny.

The fountain squirted heavenward, moonlit sprays of water flowering in mid-air, freezing there for a moment before plunging back to rejoin the calmer waters of the pond.

Chapter Twenty-Two

ROUGHLY EIGHT WEEKS AFTER CONCEPTION, Plotnick became one of the few men in the history of civilization to pretty much know what his pregnant mate was going through.

A reluctant member of the Extremely Empathic Husbands Club.

His membership became effective early one morning when he woke up in bed in his Brooklyn apartment, nauseated and pasty-faced, listening to the mechanical whir of the brick-sized device strapped to his waist that pumped toxics into a vein in his arm. A sense of doom entered his stomach, threatening to travel up his throat.

"Hey, Sonia," he weakly called, wanting her to get him a Tums. But where was she? Plotnick recalled hearing groans from her side of the bed in the wee hours as he drifted in and out of fitful sleep. Next thing he'd heard was the toilet flushing.

You can do it! Plotnick cheered himself on, standing. *I'll go there just in case.* He staggered down the hallway and jerked in a bee-line for the toilet.

Plotnick vomited. Weakly straightening, he wiped his mouth on his pajama sleeve. Just then Sonia walked into the bathroom to investigate, her face appearing as sickly and pallid as he felt.

She said nothing, gazing coldly at the yellow-orange droplets he'd left on the toilet rim. As if to demonstrate the correct method, the very next instant she vomited too, but quietly, like a British lady. She left little evidence on the porcelain ring. Then she wiped her lips with a tissue and dabbed Crest on her toothbrush.

"Daniel," she said, after gargling, in a weary, disappointed voice. "Do you know the story of Jonah? He was spit out by a whale that sneezed. Just a sneeze forced him out!"

"I'm not sure..."

"I mean, you should be afraid you may lose something you need. Like your soul."

"Oh. I see."

"You need to vomit softly. You need to be alone with your inner pig. This is what I mean."

A fresh wave of tension hit Plotnick's stomach. The last thing he frankly needed was retching lessons from a pregnant woman. "Honestly, Sonia, if my noise bothers you so much, wear those earplugs you use for my snoring," he said, forcing himself to speak gently. "What could you want more than some nice earplugs?"

"Not to be married to you?" She smiled, in a joking way. "*Escucha, mi amor.* I know you're going through a tough time. Look on the good side. Think of seven months from now— our little *bebesito* to cheer you up!"

"Thanks," Plotnick said, softening a bit too. "Maybe we're a two-lump family now."

"You shouldn't call our baby a lump. My point is, *mi amor*, we'll get through this."

"Sure we will," he said, as agreeably as he could manage.

But as Sonia handed him his toothbrush to freshen up and then exited the bathroom, leaving him alone with his bewildered reflection in the mirror, he wondered again, exactly what was this *thing* they'd get through?

Here he was, starting chemo and his wife, knocked up! His own growth was bad enough, how the hell would he take care of another? Here he was, taking poison and throwing up. He could go bald. Plotnick knew if the chemo didn't work, he might not be around to help his child grow into an adult. And the child wouldn't even be Jewish, since Sonia was Catholic and Jewishness is determined by the mother.

The way Plotnick felt now, he and Sonia had not two lumps but three. Because something else was also growing inside Plotnick. A feeling of dread. Dread his future was spinning out of control.

Plotnick scolded himself for his impulsiveness five months earlier. In the heat of the moment he'd agreed to make a child. And Sonia had latched onto the idea like a locomotive onto a caboose. He should have put his foot down when she insisted they go all out, try all sorts of methods to get pregnant. Compassionate with a pushy exterior. This was *la forma de ser* of Plotnick's wife. The form of her soul, a form Plotnick was getting way too comfortable with.

It grew worse. Their physical symptoms began to converge. The fetal heartbeat inside Sonia, to Plotnick's great and growing dismay, synchronized with the whir of the fanny pack pump fastened to his waist; as if the hormones swirling inside Sonia swam in tempo with the chemicals eroding his insides. Chemicals including Adriamycin, the toxic pillar of his anti-cancer cocktail, and Vincristine, Cytoxan, and Dacarbazine.

Plotnick desperately wanted to revoke his membership to the Extremely Empathic Husbands Club. But one morning, about to get out of the shower, he spied an odd clump of dark hair in the drain. Examining it closely, he determined it was his.

As Plotnick wrapped himself in a towel, gazing incredulously at his head in the bathroom mirror, Sonia strode up. Rolling up the bottom of her shirt, she revealed seven short black hairs sprouting around her naval.

"See? Isn't it terrible? And that's not the worst. Look." He examined her in the fluorescent light. Fresh fuzz clung to the underside of her upper neck.

"Woop-di-doo," he said, unimpressed. He pointed out his uneven scalp, then the hairball in his hands. "I've got a *patch*."

"Oh Daniel. It's happening." She placed a comforting hand on his head. "We are becoming opposites, but in a similar way!"

He felt like hissing, but instead stood there, the grim, silent husband. He was in no mood to celebrate his wife's newfound solidarity with him, and nudged away her hand. "Please, don't touch, Sonia. My hair's liable to fall out if you feel it. I'm trying to hold onto what I have."

"Look at me, Daniel. At my eyes. Good. Now, if you're worried about your bad hair, why don't you let me shave it? Think of all the sexy men who shave their head. Bruce Willis. Andre Agassi. There's no reason for my husband to look like a bad lawn."

Plotnick readjusted the hair still attached to his head, thinking gloomily of his first wife's failed attempt to help him. *Sonia's on a hormone-fueled power trip. She's hysterical. Of course, that's not all true,* he went on to himself. *Maybe I'm in denial about my hair. Sometimes she's gentle and loving.*

She cooks for me and will be an income-producing doctor in the United States one day.

"You think you're comforting me," he said, "but you're making me feel worse. Maybe I'll lose one patch and that's it. I need to hold onto that hope like my hair. For my sanity."

Sonia briefly laughed. "I'm a doctor. This is how it happens. The nurse was correct the first time."

It's cold of her to mention *the nurse*, he thought, furrowing his still-thick eyebrows. He remembered the day waiting for his first chemo treatment—how the nurse had entered the clinic's waiting room with a clipboard in her hand, pencil jammed behind her ear, snapping her gum with attitude. Her blonde hair dangling before him like a fortune-teller's bead curtain. The nurse thrust at him a directory of area wig dealers, as well as Revlon's "Pocket Guide to Hair Alternatives," which featured several dozen head shots of models donning blonde, brunette, and silver wigs.

The names of the wigs were reminiscent of American car brands, including Tempo, Mystery, Legacy. Others, with names like Casablanca, Kiev, and Sydney, topped women who seemed to hail from these exotic places. But Plotnick noticed these models' eyebrows were too full to be those of chemo patients. He realized something. *Of course!* Clearly these were healthy women with real hair under the wigs. *All fakes!* He'd bristled with annoyance. *Every last one of them.*

As Plotnick stood before the mirror in the bathroom with his wife, he touched his thinning hair to reassure himself he hadn't lost every strand. He suspected the nurse, and perhaps Sonia, were mocking him. He felt like he'd made an appointment at the barbershop from *Village of the Damned.*

Plotnick smirked. "Instead of you shaving me, why don't you let me shave the peach fuzz from your face?"

Sonia's eyes moistened with hurt.

"Don't give me your look," he said. "That's what *you* wanted to do to *me,* right? Shave me? Why can't I say the same thing to you? Fair is fair!"

She switched off the light above the mirror. "Is it fair I look like an old woman with fuzz? Is it my choice? And now you would *shave* me so it grows back as stubble? Like a man with—how do you call it?—five o'clock shadow?"

Sonia stalked out of the room, leaving him to stare in the mirror.

A bad man with bad hair. This is what I look and feel like.

That evening the two sat silently at the kitchen table gazing at boxes of Chinese takeout—moo shoo chicken and shrimp with garlic sauce. Plotnick helped himself, mixing in extra white rice to soothe his stomach. White rice felt nice and digestible.

"How about some moo shoo?" he asked. "It's like a fajita. Only Chinese." He made her one, brushing some sauce on the tortilla and filling it with stir-fried vegetables and chicken.

She stared at the fajita. Pushing away the plate, she stood. "I'm so tired, Daniel. All this grease ... Sorry, *mi amor.*" She left and went to bed, leaving him to dine alone.

As he struggled to keep down his food, a dark thought seeped into him. People were starving in his home. His own family.

Fact is, her nausea was worse than his. The next morning she skipped breakfast except for coffee, into which she oddly dunked a few mozzarella strings. She picked at lunch. Dinner was a couple of sweet rolls. More coffee. Plotnick could picture his bony, nascent child locked in a moist, pinkish room, jittery as a puppy lapping espresso.

Something flashed through him, a flash of paternal protectiveness that flickered on and off and then stayed on for a while. For the first time, the cancer patient fretted more about the clump of cells living in his wife's body than the lump he harbored in his. *Shouldn't pregnant people eat twice as much?* Plotnick worried. *Instead of half as much?*

He researched his wife's condition over the Internet, struggling to comfort himself with facts. He learned about hormones, the feminine mystique, and philosophy. He considered the economic theory that creation and destruction are indelibly linked, seeds of growth sown in the wreckage of the old order. He clicked on a pregnancy website, learning that the hormone causing Sonia to puke also nourished the fetus by diverting nutrients from the mother's bloodstream. Called "human chorionic gonadotrophin" (HCG), it sparks the placenta's growth. But by diverting insulin to the developing fetus, HCG upsets the mother's ability to absorb fat and sugar, creating a nutrient bottleneck. Sweets and grease, their mere smells, can nauseate the mother.

Plotnick went to Barnes & Noble after work. He read of historical precedents, how extreme diets among societal leaders provoked the rise and fall of great cultures. The Holy Roman Empire flourished on gluttony, and French gourmands came to rule haute cuisine. Russian czars stumbled on bad sausage. The big mystery was the rise in Ethiopian restaurants in Lower Manhattan. Didn't they have mass starvation there? But Plotnick ultimately drew scant comfort from the planet's larger malnourished community. More practically, he found a book that might be useful for Sonia—*The Wise Woman's Childbearing Year,* which offered natural remedies to pregnancy-induced nausea. "Drink a tea made from dried peach leaves," it advised female readers, though giving few clues as to where to actually get this item. "Eat unsalted crackers of matzo before getting out of bed." Sip a "raspberry infusion."

Something about the "wise woman" part clicked with Plotnick. Wasn't Sonia wise? His own medical sojourn had instilled in him a grudging respect for medical professionals, particularly one with the wisdom of an immigrant.

Following the book's instructions one afternoon, he prepared a glass of apple-cider vinegar mixed with warm water, praised in chapter two as a stomach remedy. He cubed tofu, a greaseless protein, arranging them next to the glass of vinegar. Surely she'd appreciate what he'd done for her, for their baby. He eagerly carried the tray and halted at the doorway of their bedroom, silently peeking at his wife.

A tear-streaked Sonia lay on the bed, not noticing him as he watched from across the room. Her shirt was pulled up. Her hands rested on her bare swollen stomach. "*Mi bebé,*" she said softly. "*Mio.*"

He heard nurturing but also loneliness in her voice, as if only she cared for this unborn child. Plotnick came up and placed his hand on top of the one she'd placed over her stomach. "You okay?"

"*Gracias,* Daniel. I'm fine." She saw the tray in his hands. "What's this?"

"Er, lunch."

Her face tensing over the small white cubes. "You are feeding me dice?"

"Would you prefer a sip of warm vinegar?"

She glared at him.

"Listen," he said, defensively. "This book I bought recommends all-natural foods..."

His voice trailed off as Sonia fiddled with the tofu knife, prompting him to back up a few inches. An even-tempered Latin female will, during ordinary conversation, wave a knife in the air while discussing how to broil a chicken. Put her on hormones, and...

"I want to help you," he insisted. "You've got the medical boards to study for and you haven't touched a book in weeks. He's our child! He needs to eat, and you, your body, is the only restaurant in town."

"Don't worry. Our baby is half me. She's tough. And she doesn't like dice. You should maybe feed her something Colombian instead." She smiled. "You see, Daniel, now you know how I feel when you don't let me help by shaving you. Now you are the person I was. It is my body. Sorry if I sound selfish. But I cannot tell my body to want something it doesn't; the same way you stopped me from helping yours."

He didn't quite understand her point, but sensed it was a good one. Wasn't marriage like this? Bursts of honesty punctuated by light years of distance? "I sort of get what you mean," Plotnick said. "But you need to stop using our future child's health to make a point." He deftly grabbed the knife out of her hand, picked up the plate of uneaten food, and strode out of the room. Then for some reason he turned.

From the hallway, he could see Sonia facing the bedroom wall, her back to him like an icy fortress. *Is this what having cancer is about?* Was he trying to poison himself before he poisoned his marriage?

As Plotnick listened to his own footsteps moving away from Sonia, he felt stuck in yet another downward marital spiral, as if the tests he and Sonia individually and regularly underwent were monitoring their slow separate declines.

Just a day earlier, Plotnick had endured his monthly "Muga-Scan," a nuclear chemical injected into his vein to check for heart damage from Adriamycin, which disrupted heart rhythms in some recipients. The doctor stuck him with yet another needle, this time drawing blood to test his resilience to his three other chemo drugs, which suppressed bone marrow production of white blood cells, the body's defense against getting sick. They even checked him for side effects to side effects. To replenish his depleted white blood cells, Plotnick had started taking Neupogen, but the drug also caused flu-like aches in the bones, which required him to take aspirin. And so on and so forth.

Sonia, in addition to regular checkups by her OBGYN, underwent regular sonograms to check the fetus's heartbeat, breathing, and developmental rate. But Sonia herself appeared anything but vital. As the weeks progressed, she went from eating like a bird to eating almost nothing. She spent mornings and part of afternoons in bed, reading Spanish-language romance novels, watching Colombian-made soap operas on Telemundo TV, and talking to her stomach bulge.

Plotnick had nightmares about lump reversal, Sonia giving birth to a tumor, a fetus surgically removed from Plotnick's throat. After one such dream Plotnick, awakened from a nap by his own sleep-muttering and sick to his stomach, put on his coat and shoes and a baseball cap. By this point his hair had taken on the characteristics of a neglected, grub-infested lawn. He was famished, nauseated, and dizzy.

He went down the apartment stairs into the fresh spring morning air; there was a softness to the light. The air, fragrant with flowering trees, rose to him on a breeze, reviving him a bit. Plotnick strolled past the varied culinary establishments along Park Slope's gentrified Seventh Avenue. Scents of Italian food floated by, making him gag; he saw children in strollers grasping lollipops and could nearly taste the sickening sweetness.

He stopped at a café and ordered a cappuccino to go, took one sip, and spilled it out on the street. Watching the brown, foamy liquid flow down a sewer grate, he tried to cheer himself up about the choices he'd made in life. He recalled the cross-cultural food humor he and Sonia shared early on in their relationship, before chemo made everything seem infinitely unfunny. "Some place your America is," she once poked at him. "You get a big bag of juicy mangos for two dollars in Colombia, but you pay two thirty for a single hard green mango at Pathmark."

"Yeah," he replied, "but those six hundred dollar plane tickets you need to fly them in from Colombia really add to the cost."

Sonia's wit, sharp as a coffee bean picker's machete; his own, pungent as gefilte fish. And the current cancer situation *did* seem funny, when Plotnick thought hard on it. He could imagine sharing a laugh over how they might get "a group rate on lumpectomies." Maybe their growths would remind them why they were together. Opposites attract, right? Hadn't this been his motto?

Clearly, Plotnick's lump was bad, hers good. She wanted to nurture her growth much as he strived to murder his. Just as their different personalities drew them to each other, Plotnick hoped their opposing lumps could help deepen their relationship.

He stopped staring at the coffee going down the sewer grate and resumed walking. He came to a bodega with an outdoor display of green *platanos*. What was it she'd once asked for? A lifetime ago? Bimbo. The crunchy bread favored by Latinos. For some reason, the brand name was American slang for a stupid beautiful woman. He'd tasted it once. Like Melba toast, it crunched so loudly in your mouth you couldn't hear your own thoughts. He frankly never understood the adult appeal of a pre-toasted bread seemingly made for teething infants.

But maybe his hormone-crazed wife would go for it. He ducked in the small cluttered store which reeked of overripe bananas and saw the familiar red-and-blue packages—"*Con Buen Gusto!*"—stacked next to the cigarette displays and coconut cookies and squares of guava paste wrapped in wax paper. He grabbed a loaf (and, on a whim, a pack of disposable razors), handing the money to a cashier who grasped just enough English to make change.

He returned to the apartment. "I brought you something," he announced to Sonia. It was a Saturday afternoon; Sonia, still in bed instead of studying for the medical boards, groggily rubbed her eyes. "Bimbo," he said. "And no, I'm not calling you one. I mean, dear, you are the opposite of a Bimbo."

She silently gazed at the package of bread. For a full minute, neither of them said anything. Then Plotnick uttered the only four-syllable Spanish word he knew.

"*Mantequilla?*" he asked.

She nodded. Plotnick went to the kitchen and brought back a stick of butter and spread some across a slice for her, handing it to her.

Shutting her eyes as if dreaming, Sonia crunched down.

"Oh," she said, savoring the mouthful. "You are trying to feed our child Colombian food! Wait till I tell my mother about this."

"I bought this at a bodega on Fifth Street," he reminded her. "It's made in a bakery somewhere, probably by Latinos, but can't swear any of the bakers are from your country...."

"Do not ruin my dream, *mi amor.*" She opened her eyes. "I can remember the food of my country so clearly. Eating Bimbo for breakfast every Sunday with my mother and father and sister and brothers. And the fruits! In Colombia, the papayas and *guanabanas* are so ripe and sweet and large. You buy them from people on the street while waiting in traffic in my city. Sitting in my car, I could grab a mango with both hands to squeeze the juice into my mouth."

Plotnick was struck by an urge to make fun of his wife. "I didn't know Colombia had traffic lights!" or some such joke making fun of less-developed nations, but her nostalgic face made him tread carefully.

She continued, "I remember so clearly now. The time I was eight years old. I was in the country with some friends, and there were all these pineapples growing in the field along the road. We walked down the dirt road and asked the owner if we could have a pineapple. And he said—" She turned away from Plotnick as if he embodied the owner. "—he said no. Just like I can't eat all the things I enjoy now because my stomach will not allow me."

Plotnick thought she might start to cry, but instead she said, "Those were the happiest times of my life."

"Have another slice," he urged her.

She savored a second piece of the Melba-like toast. "You should try one," she said.

Plotnick accepted half from her and crunched down hard. Saliva squirted into his mouth. "Maybe there's something to this Bimbo," he said, swallowing.

"Right? Oh. I need to tell you the dream I had last night," Sonia said. "Actually a nightmare. My father was in it. I was walking in a beautiful forest, eating chicken … Then … then I realized I was eating the bones of my father. But I kept eating because I was so hungry. It was this horrible morning sickness."

Sonia's eyes moistened; Plotnick's jaw stopped right when it was about to crunch down on more Bimbo. He thought, *Wow. Eating feels like death for her.*

Maybe for both of us.

Struck by a sudden wave of empathy, he placed his hand on top of Sonia's. "Listen, I've been thinking…"

Plotnick handed her a disposable razor he'd bought in the bodega along with the Bimbo.

Chapter Twenty-Three

FOR A LONG MOMENT SONIA GAZED INQUISITIVELY at him.

A smile lit up her face. Without warning, she grabbed his wrist and dragged him to the bathroom. "Sit on the toilet," she commanded. She ran the water warm and splashed it across his patchy scalp. She sprayed foam from her leg-shaving kit into her hands, rubbing it between her cupped palms.

She spread the foam across his scalp. For the next twenty minutes she delicately stroked the razor across his undulating skin, the bumps, every minor indentation, the whole thing, gently as a mother bird preening its fledgling.

Finally she wiped his scalp with a damp cloth and blew off his stubble from the razor.

"Gracias," she said, kissing his smooth scalp, "for letting me do this."

He refused to peek at the mirror. He felt paralyzed. Taking a deep breath, he gazed at his reflection. *Jeez. I look like the Egghead from the original Batman TV series.* But Plotnick ran a hand over his scalp and felt, in time, he was touching someone else's smooth skull, one belonging to someone okay with the situation, not confused and embittered by it. He felt aerodynamic.

Sonia said, "I needed to do that. I felt I was living with a sick person. Now you are handsome!"

"Please address me as Bruce," he joked, a bit shakily. "As in Willis." He tried to calm himself by thinking things through. *She needs to nurture her sick neurotic husband, because if you can take care of your special-needs husband, your helpless unborn child should be a cinch.*

In that moment, Sonia seemed to him supremely confident. A talented beautician. Maybe the lump inside her could have a one-on-one conversation with Plotnick's, breaking the communications barrier. He could imagine a tête-à-tête between their lumps—his, a potential murderer; hers bearing the unborn innocence of Gandhi. His own growth might speak gruffly, Sonia's replying with a shrill naiveté born of an empowering feminine past.

Sonia gratefully handed him a booklet, *The Food Lover's Chemo Guide.* "I've been meaning to give this to you for the longest time. I was afraid you'd think I was—how do you say?—hypercrite. Telling you how to eat when I wouldn't eat myself."

"Hypocrite," Plotnick corrected. He flipped through the booklet and read out loud. "Eat foods cold or at room temperature so you won't be bothered by strong smells. If nausea is a problem, try eating dry foods like toast, cereal, or crackers before getting up. Do not try this if you are troubled by a lack of saliva."

He looked into Sonia's caring face and knew she wanted to help him. He remembered his first wife's attempts to improve his diet, and his eyes misted over. *Sometimes it's okay to let someone help you get better.* All this time he thought Judy left him because she couldn't deal with his cancer, that her attempts to nourish him were a sign of weakness. That she couldn't cope. *No. I left her because I couldn't cope.* He felt sorry he was so hard on Judy. Still, he knew she wasn't the right woman, like Sonia.

"You okay?" Sonia asked.

"Yeah. I'm fine. Listen, thanks for trying. I mean it," he said. "But this booklet reminds me of the one I read for your morning sickness advice. Remarkably similar, in fact."

"And what bad advice it was!" Sonia grabbed back the book. "Sorry. I really want to give you something. To say *gracias.* Something you'd really enjoy."

Thinking for a moment, she said, "I know! Sex without condom."

"But you said I wasn't supposed to drink liquor while I'm on chemo."

Sonia laughed. "Sex without condom is not a mixed drink!"

She shucked her shirt to demonstrate what it was. Her progesterone-swollen breasts sprung forth, tipped by nipples dark as Hershey's Kisses—yet another result, Plotnick suspected, of the pregnancy hormones surging through his wife.

Keeping her pants on for now, Sonia pushed Plotnick down to the bed, rolled him over to face her, and straddled his thighs. Her swollen abdomen hit his crotch like a basketball slamming a backboard. "Good news, honey," she said. "This time you don't need to worry about getting me pregnant."

"Are you nuts?" Plotnick said, when he realized what was going on. "The baby's going to get a black eye!"

Plotnick tried to push her off, gently—after all, they hadn't had sex since Sonia's stomach was merely an overstuffed Nerf ball—but Sonia held her position, shaking her head willfully. She reached across him to her night table for her dog-eared copy of *The Obstetrician's Illustrated Guide to Intimacy,* flipping to the "Adaptable Amniotic Fluid" chapter. As she sat there half naked, straddling Plotnick and playfully rotating her hips as if warming up her pitcher's arm for the bottom of the ninth inning of the World Series, she read aloud of the "yawning differences" during pregnancy between "rough gestational sex" and "thoughtful love-making." Even late-term fetuses could safely swish around in the mother's "Cadillac DeVille for potholes," the book confidently claimed.

"What about brain damage?" Plotnick pressed on, with weakening defenses, as his wife unzipped his fly.

Sonia gazed at him with the patience of Job, tickled his chest hairs, and flipped onward to chapter ten, which contended the true danger of sex to fetuses was contained in the semen—a male hormone called prostaglandin that could trigger premature labor in the mother.

Another gestation bible appeared in her hand, *What to Expect When You're Expecting.* As Sonia fiddled with his shirt buttons, he grew distracted by his wife's astounding ability to multi-task. She read on, "If you get a green light [from your OBGYN], then by all means go ahead if you feel a desire and feel comfortable with it. But if the traffic light is red … then foster intimacy in other ways." Candlelit restaurant and walking hand-in-hand in Central Park were two suggestions.

"Do not discuss sex with parents. Or mother-in-law. This can have the opposite effect," she said, proudly ad-libbing. "What you think? Do you like my humor, husband? Hey. Are you even alive?"

Lying there, Plotnick wasn't sure. He wasn't in the mood for humor, sex, or even humorous sex. Certainly he had less sexual drive than his wife, who'd evidently refueled her tank by eating all those Bimbos.

"My poor, dear man," she said, climbing off him.

"Then you see what I mean?"

"No, I don't know what you mean. Why don't you tell me?"

"I mean, there's a lot in this stomach of yours. It's so hard, how can there *not* be something living in there? How can we *not* be worried about it?"

"I'm happy you recognize there is a baby in me. But, let's have sex."

"I lost the feeling. If I ever had it." Did he feel his eyes welling up? How embarrassing! Maybe he cared *too* much.

"Shut up, dear." She touched a finger to his wet cheek, and touched the same finger to his chest, near his heart. "You've got something inside you too. And we're taking care of that."

"You mean, poisoning it with chemo."

"Sure. But why don't we make them touch?"

"Uh…"

"They can kiss. You know, make up. Or maybe they will attack each other. You never know. In your American Land of Opportunity, anything is possible. Sex is really the only time two private parts can touch."

He pondered this new thought: *Touché!* Cut the small talk and have a biting contest! May the bravest win!

A way to toughen the little guy up. Or her. For the real world.

"Well?" Sonia said. "Do not—how do you Americans say?—dally-dilly."

"It's dilly…" But Sonia had already grabbed Plotnick's naked waist with two impatient hands, as if ready to squeeze juice from a papaya. "It's dilly-dally," he tried to say again. But she'd shucked her pants and now pressed hard against him, gyrating her hips like a meat grinder struck into sudden awareness.

It was over in three seconds.

The nude, international couple lay there staring at the ceiling. Dazed. Spent. Silent. In the vague light one appeared like a beached dolphin with a tan; the other, faint and hairless, a dead ringer for a giant albino mole.

"Well, there's mud in the baby's eye," Plotnick said.

"Then the two bumps kiss and make up," she sort of agreed.

"Guess it was a tie," Plotnick said. "I mean, the two of them were in the ring, and it was a good fight. Like the Pillsbury Dough Boy meets a giant zit."

"You are this giant zit?"

"Actually the other way around. But let's not go there."

She gazed at him with soothing eyes. "Don't worry. Let's call it a tie, *mi amor,*" she said.

"A tie. Got it."

"I mean, no more *loco*. From you. Cut the craziness. I don't want you saying, 'I don't want a baby no more.'"

"'Never more,' spake the raven. 'Never more.'"

"Who is this raven? Your mistress?" she joked.

"Uh…"

"Anyway, we are the lump family now. *Señor* and *Señora* Lump. And *Bambina* Lump. Like it or not, husband!"

Chapter Twenty-Four

Sonia gave birth by Caesarian to a healthy girl, Plotnick's cancer spread further despite the chemo and, with the religious conviction of an octogenarian Jew cramming for the finals, he decided to give his child a ritualistic mikvah to make her Jewish.

Of course, he wasn't really dying. Not yet. The cancer grew slowly. He felt sick from the chemo not the cancer. But he couldn't ignore his own physical condition: by the time the baby, Rachel, was eight months old, even Plotnick's eyebrows were bald. He'd lost weight along with his appetite. Who knew what would conk out next.

So one afternoon in upper Manhattan, a small crowd—Sonia, Plotnick's mother and father, Mona, Steve, and two rabbis, one conservative, one reform—answered the clarion call of eleventh-hour religious conviction. They gathered around a small pool of lukewarm chlorinated water as Plotnick removed his shirt and waded in, clasping his daughter to his bony chest.

He was to let her go. Literally. Like God commanded Adam and Eve to go from the Garden of Eden. Like Moses beseeched Pharaoh, "Let my people go!" Now, letting his own child go in the year 2001, Plotnick would practically write his own Bible chapter. Whoever thought of this sadistic ritual, he mused as he stood there, suspending Rachel above the waist-high water, probably no one remembered from Adam.

She clung to his neck as he peered through the haze of steam at the pair of rabbis. "How long does she need to stay under?" he asked again.

"Three seconds," the reform rabbi said.

"God willing," the conservative one added.

"Maybe four seconds," the first rabbi went on.

The rabbis checked their stopwatches. A collective hush rose in the tiled room. "You can do it, kid!" Steve said.

"*Buena suerte, mi familia,*" Sonia said. Good luck, my family.

Inhaling as if he himself were about to go under, Plotnick unclasped his hands, letting the baby slip through them. Her tiny fingers twitched up briefly through the surface. Eyes dimmed into robin eggs. She seemed to wave good-bye as she sank.

A gasp escaped his wife. Or perhaps himself. *She's helpless. And I can't help her.*

Time trickled by, each second a leap year. By some automatic reflex, Plotnick reached into the water and scooped up Rachel, clamping her to his chest.

"She's okay!" Steve announced through the din of her screams. Plotnick's family relaxed. But the rabbis checked their stopwatches and smiled sadly. Not enough time had passed.

Do they want my blood? Is this even worth the trouble? Giving his daughter a mikvah didn't make sense, after all, if he didn't last for the Bat Mitzvah. Maybe he'd make her a Buddhist instead. But something inside him grew solid as the Ten Commandments. If his orthodox grandfather could refrain from pork every day of his ninety-three years until death, Plotnick could forgo feeling safe for three or four seconds.

As Rachel's protests softened to whimpers, Plotnick dropped her back. Splosh!

Her little body wavered in the water. Then her fingers broke back through the surface and grabbed his arm.

Screams blasted the room as he snatched her up again.

The rabbis checked their stopwatch, shaking their heads.

At least she's a fast learner, he thought wearily. *Smart enough to grab onto me.*

Like a depleted runner in the last mile of the marathon, nearly questioning the existence of God, Plotnick dropped his child a third time.

He moved backward two steps, out of her reach.

She went down, slipping away.

Plotnick's eyes misted over, vision blurring. He flashed back to the moment of his own terrifying plunge. He saw not his daughter sinking, but the hulking shadow of the GW Bridge on the Hudson River. White-winged birds swooped low, screaming, as wind whistled through his nose ring. Pock pock pock went the helicopter floating past.

"Daniel!" Sonia said sharply.

Plotnick snapped to attention and saw his daughter sinking like a rag doll. Weakness coursed through him, his bones filled with jelly, but he dove straight down, as Sonia also jumped in.

Father and mother jetted down like one person and grabbed Rachel and snatched her from the pool bottom.

The three broke through the surface like a twisted triplet of Seaworld dolphins, exploding into empty air.

Plotnick gasped for breath, but Rachel relaxed in his arms. Alarmed, Sonia slapped her daughter's back. Once, twice. Thrice. Then—

Cah! Cah! Rachel spit up. Cah! She drooled water out of the side of her mouth. Cah! She was breathing evenly again and smiling, not at all upset, despite her hyperventilating father, her weeping grateful mother holding her.

Plotnick's mother and father and Mona and Steve broke into relieved applause. The rabbis beamed. "Three seconds," the first one said. "Maybe four."

"For both of you," the other said.

"You mean…" Plotnick stammered.

"Yes," the two rabbis said.

"…both Sonia and Rachel?"

"Yes. The whole family! We'll make a special exception for Sonia, if she wants. When you save another life, it is as if you save your own. This is the essence of Judaism. Welcome to the faith."

"I … accept!" Sonia said, adding a prayer of gratitude to her special Catholic saint, while Rachel, tired from all the excitement, slept with scrunched face against her mother's bosom, corners of her lips upraised angelically.

Plotnick also closed his eyes. If it ended with this little girl against his wife's milk-swollen breast, he was cool with that. Steve slapping his old man on the back. His mother cooing into the baby's ear. If things ended here, that would be enough.

But in fact, this isn't how it ends. Daniel Plotnick goes on to write a novel. He tries a new cancer drug, with fewer side effects, that holds his disease at bay. His daughter looks up to him, and his wife opens her own medical practice. They live in a spacious house in upstate New York instead of the claustrophobic fourth-floor walk-up in Brooklyn. They sow seeds in a little garden plot, weed tomato plants, and set down aluminum pie plates filled with Budweiser to drown the slugs. Each morning he walks his two small dogs unleashed, like his thoughts, through a nearby forest.

One day, Plotnick publishes his novel. And he knows he's just getting started.

Acknowledgments

THIS BOOK IS A WORK OF FICTION. AS FICTION authors do, I drew for material from my own experience, and went to town with it. My overriding goal was to create a fully realized story, with drama, comedy, and a narrative arc. Toward that end, the characters I invented to populate my story are precisely that—invented. Any perceived resemblances to real people are coincidental to my goals as a novelist.

Here's the truth. My father and mother were supportive during my marriage and health struggles, and my road toward renewal. My father, who in fact never pushed me off a bridge, showed up when I needed him. My mother, who in fact does not talk like a Yiddisha, is the artist in my family who encouraged my writing ever since I wrote my first poem in kindergarten. So my first acknowledgment goes to my parents as well as to my brother and sister. Thanks.

I'd be terribly remiss if I didn't thank my teachers at Bennington College Writing Seminars, who taught me to believe in myself and seek the truth in my fiction. Thank you, Alice Mattison, Askold Melnyczuk, Virgil Suarez, and Martha Cooley.

I'm grateful to my fellow survivors of medullary thyroid cancer, whose stories of perseverance helped strengthen my own.

To my trusty readers, especially Amy Burton, Nina Dabek, Lale Davidson, Richard Gotti, and Jan Johnson. I apologize to anyone I left out. My book would be a lot shabbier without you.

To editor Summer Ross, for your expertise and time in polishing the novel, and the rest of the crew at WiDō Publishing, especially Karen Gowan, who guided me through the publishing effort. To Steven Novak, for his whimsical cover design, and my pal Kenny Funk for crucial last-minute help on the typeface. Seth Kaufman, Clea Simon, and fellow WiDō authors—whose wise counsel guided me when I didn't know where else to turn. David Siff, wherever you are, who so many years ago talked me into writing a book.

I must acknowledge all those senders of rejection slips I amassed over thirteen years of writing this novel. For without rejection, there is no acceptance.

Most of all, I thank my wife Ingrid and daughter Sophie, who put up with the entire ordeal, my tens of thousands of hours spent isolated behind my manuscript, who supported me in more ways than even Daniel Plotnick could imagine. Nothing would be possible without you.

Questions and Topics for Discussion

1. Author David Kalish chooses a comedic tone to tell a serious story of cancer, divorce, and renewal. Why do you think he opted for humor? How would your reading experience differ if the book was written in a straightforward style, such as first-person memoir? Would you be more or less engrossed in the story?

2. Can you picture yourself using comedy to write about your own personal troubles? How do you imagine that experience feeling? Would humor help or hurt your ability to write about trauma?

3. People react in countless ways to serious illness in their lives. How does Daniel Plotnick respond to his cancer diagnosis? Do his actions make him more likeable or less likable as a person? Have you ever encountered a reaction as extreme as his, and if so, what similarities do you see between that person and Daniel?

4. How would you say Daniel changed during the course of the book? Is he more in touch with his feelings at the end than at the beginning? If so, does his progression deepen your understanding of him as a character?

5. Some marriages grow stronger when a spouse becomes seriously ill, but others weaken. Why do you think

Daniel's first marriage collapsed whereas his second succeeded? How did the personalities of his wives, Judy and Sonia, contribute to these divergent outcomes?

6. After Daniel goes gothic and comes home dressed in black with a ring through his nose, his first wife Judy tells him she feels like "part of me is dying." What does she mean by that? How does Judy's own troubled past shape her attitude toward her sick husband?

7. Close friends can provide critical emotional support to people going through hard times. How does Steve console and comfort his buddy Daniel? Does he help, or hurt? Can you imagine reacting in a similar way to news, say, of a friend's serious illness? If not, how do you see yourself reacting?

8. Even for adults, having a parent who understands the tough times you're going through can make a big difference. Do you think Daniel's father understood his problems? Does he provide the support his son needs? Why or why not?

9. Sonia finds out Daniel has cancer on their first date. How would you describe her reaction? Does Sonia's personal history help her cope with Daniel's disease—and if so, how?

10. Frustrated by her inability to become pregnant, Sonia tells Daniel he needs to make up with his father in order to become a father himself. "A child is conceived when the man is ready to be a father," she says. What do you think she means by this? By the end of the book, does Daniel come to accept this philosophy on some level?

11. How does Daniel's growth into a parent affect his vision of the world and his ability to cope with his mortality? Do you think Rachel's mikvah brings his evolution full circle?

12. What kind of note does the book end on? Hopeful or sad?

13. The author frames the book in the concept of "opposites." How does this narrative frame help hold the book together and drive the narrative forward? Does Daniel's obsession with opposites gain momentum as the book progresses?

14. Did the book expand your range of experience or challenge your assumptions? Did it take you to a place you haven't been before or help you see a place you know in a different light? Did reading it help you to understand a person better—perhaps a friend or relative, even yourself?

CPSIA information can be obtained at www.ICGtesting.com
Printed in the USA
BVOW08s2332240214

345906BV00006B/22/P